MW00790818

HELLO,
GOODBYE,
AND
EVERYTHING
IN BETWEEN

HELLO, GOODBYE, AND EVERYTHING
IN BETWEEN

JENNIFER E. SMITH

poppy

Little, Brown and Company
New York Boston

Also by Jennifer E. Smith:
The Geography of You and Me
This Is What Happy Looks Like
The Statistical Probability of Love at First Sight
The Storm Makers
You Are Here
The Comeback Season

Copyright © 2015 by Jennifer E. Smith Inc.

Poppy

Hachette Book Group
1290 Avenue of the Americas, New York, NY 10104
Visit us at lb-teens.com

Poppy is an imprint of Little, Brown and Company.
The Poppy name and logo are trademarks of Hachette Book Group, Inc.

The publisher is not responsible for websites (or their content)
that are not owned by the publisher.

First Edition: September 2015

Library of Congress Cataloging-in-Publication Data

Smith, Jennifer E., 1980–
Hello, goodbye, and everything in between / Jennifer E. Smith. — First edition.
pages cm
Summary: High school sweethearts Clare and Aidan spend the night before they leave for college reminiscing about their relationship and deciding whether they should stay together or break up.
ISBN 978-0-316-33442-6 (hardcover) — ISBN 978-0-316-33444-0 (ebook) — ISBN 978-0-316-33445-7 (library edition ebook) [1. Dating (Social customs)—Fiction. 2. Love—Fiction.] I. Title.
PZ7.S65141He 2015 [Fic]—dc23 2014043210

10 9 8 7 6 5 4 3 2 1

RRD-C

Printed in the United States of America

To Jenn, with a whole lot of gratitude

PROLOGUE

When Aidan opens the door, Clare rises onto her tiptoes to kiss him, and for a moment, it feels like any other night.

"Hi," she says, once she's stepped back again, and he smiles. "Hi."

They stare at each other for a few long seconds, neither quite sure how to begin.

"So," Clare says eventually.

Aidan attempts a smile. "So."

"I guess this is it."

He nods. "I guess it is."

"The last night," she says, and he tilts his head at her.

"You know it doesn't have to be."

"Aidan..."

"I know, I know," he says, holding up his hands. "But you can't really blame me, right? I've still got a little bit of time to change your mind."

"Only twelve hours," she says, glancing at her watch. "I can't believe that's all we have left."

"And that's only if we don't sleep."

"We're definitely not wasting any time on sleep," she tells him, pulling a folded piece of notebook paper from the pocket of her dress. "We have way too much to do."

Aidan raises an eyebrow. "That'd better not be a list of reasons why we should break up...."

"It's not," she says as she hands it over to him, watching as he scans the page with a bemused expression. "I just figured maybe we could use a plan."

"And this is it?"

She nods. "This is it."

"Okay," he says, taking a deep breath. "Then I guess we should get going."

Together, they start to walk in the direction of the car, but halfway there, Clare stops short, suddenly and unaccountably nervous, her heart drumming hard in her chest. She looks over at Aidan with slightly panicked eyes. "This is kind of crazy, isn't it?"

"What?" he asks.

"That we leave tomorrow," she says, her voice rising a little. "That after all this time, we only have twelve hours left. I mean...we're finally here, you know? At the end of the road."

"Or," he reminds her, "the beginning."

Clare doesn't say anything; she wants desperately to believe him, but standing here on the edge of something so big, it seems impossible.

"Trust me," Aidan says, reaching for her hand. "A lot can happen in twelve hours."

STOP #1

The High School

6:24 PM

In the car, Aidan pauses before turning the key in the ignition, and for a brief second, Clare lets herself imagine that they're on their way out to dinner or a movie, or anywhere, really, even just the kind of aimless, purposeless drive that's been the only thing on the agenda so many times before. Their nights always seem to begin in this way: the two of them sitting in Aidan's dusty Volvo, trying to decide what to do.

But tonight is different.

It's not a beginning at all. Tonight is an ending.

Aidan's hand is still hovering over the keys, and Clare glances down at the piece of notebook paper on her lap. During the short walk over to the Gallaghers' house—a walk she's made about a thousand times in the past two years—she folded and refolded the page so many times that it's already soft and wrinkled.

"Maybe we should just take off or something," Aidan says, looking at her sideways. "Just keep driving till we hit Canada."

"Canada, huh?" Clare says, raising her eyebrows. "Are we going on the lam?"

He shrugs. "Fine. Maybe just Wisconsin, then."

She reaches over, resting a hand on the back of his neck, where his reddish hair is newly trimmed, cut close in a way that makes him look older somehow. "I'm leaving first thing in the morning," she says gently. "The car's already packed. And your flight's at noon."

"I know," he says, but he won't look at her. His eyes are fixed on the closed door of the garage. "That's my point. Let's skip it all."

"College?" she says with a smile, letting her hand drop.

"Yeah," he says, nodding now. "Who needs it? Let's run away together instead. Just for a year or so. We'll start a new life. In the country. Or better yet, a deserted island."

"You *would* look nice in a hula skirt."

"I'm serious," he says, though she knows he's not. He's just desperate and sad, nervous and excited, wildly unsure of everything as they barrel toward the invisible line that will separate their lives into a before and an after. Same as her.

"Aidan," she says quietly, and this time, his eyes find hers. "This is happening. Tomorrow. No matter what."

"I know," he admits.

"Which is why we have to figure out what to do about it."

"Right, but—"

"Nope," she says, cutting him off. She holds up the piece of paper. "No more talking. We've been talking all

4

summer, and it's gotten us nowhere. We've just been going around in circles: Stay together, break up, stay together, break up. . . ."

"Stay together," Aidan finishes, grinning a little.

Clare laughs. "The point is that we're hopeless. So no more talking. For now, let's just drive, okay?"

He leans forward, reaching for the keys, and then turns over the engine.

"Okay," he says.

Their first stop isn't far away, and they drive in silence, all the familiar sights of the town slipping by outside the window: the bridge over the ravine, the road lined with pine trees, the gazebo in the park. Clare tries to absorb each one of them as they whip past, because by the time she returns at Thanksgiving, she knows she might be someone entirely different, and she suspects that—because of that—all this might look different, too. And something about that scares her. So one by one, she tries to pin them in place: each tree, each road, each house.

This is how it all started this morning, when she woke up in a panic about how many goodbyes she still had to say. Not just the people: Aidan, of course; and her best friend, Stella; Aidan's sister, Riley; and his pal, Scotty; plus the handful of their other friends who are still around.

But there was also the town itself. All the landmarks that had been the background to her childhood. She couldn't leave without going to the village green one more time, or getting one last slice of pizza at their favorite spot.

She couldn't possibly take off without one more trip to the beach, one final party, one last drive past the high school.

And so she made a list. But it didn't take long for her to realize that most of the things that meant something to her were inextricably tied to Aidan. This place was a ghost town of sorts, littered with milestones and memories from their nearly two-year relationship.

So it had turned into something else, this night: a nostalgia tour, a journey into the past, a walk down memory lane. It would be a way for her to say goodbye to this town where she'd lived her whole life, and maybe—somehow—to Aidan, too.

She can't help shivering a little at the thought of this, and she presses the button on the car door, closing her window.

Aidan glances over. "Too windy?" he asks, rolling up his own window, and she nods. But it's more than that. It's the same icy dread that fills her each time she starts to imagine it; not just the goodbye, but everything that's to come afterward: the hurt that will surely trail them to opposite coasts, so strong that she can already feel it even now, when he's only inches away.

The truth is, she's still waiting for her heart to get on board with the decision her head has made. But she's running out of time.

When they reach the long drive leading up to the high school, Aidan frowns. "So tell me," he says as they pull up to the front of the sprawling building and into one of the empty parking spots. "Why exactly are we here?"

It's early evening on a Friday toward the end of August, and the school sits hushed and empty. Though she spent four years here, Clare's already having trouble remembering the feel of the place when it's full of students, everyone spilling out the wooden doors and onto the front lawn. It's only been two months, but somehow, all that seems like a very long time ago.

"Because," she says, turning to Aidan, "it's the first stop on the list."

"I know *that*," he says. "But how come?"

"It's where we met," she explains as she gets out of the car. "And the idea is to start at the beginning."

"So this is a *chronological* scavenger hunt, then."

"It's not a scavenger hunt at all. Think of it more like a refresher course."

"A refresher course in what?"

She smiles at him over the top of the car. "Us."

"So kind of like our greatest hits," he says, twirling the keys on his finger as he walks around to her, and for a moment, it's like none of the rest of it happened. Just now, just for this second, he's not the person she knows best in the world, but the new kid again, the one who'd shown up on the very first day of junior year, all red hair and freckles and ridiculous height, appearing out of nowhere and turning her inside out.

The slanted light is at his back, forcing Clare to squint as she studies him for a few long seconds. "Did I ever tell you," she says, "that I used to be late to English every

7

single day, just so I could bump into you on your way to Pre-calc?"

"Well, now I feel kind of bad," Aidan says, his eyes creasing at the corners. "If I'd known *that*, I would've tried to be more punctual."

"It wouldn't have mattered," she says, remembering the way he used to come loping around the corner, his books tucked under his arm like a football, always missing the bell, at first because he'd get lost, and later because he'd always manage to lose track of time. "I would've waited all day. I probably would've waited forever."

She's not serious, of course, but there's something wistful in his smile.

"Yeah?" he says.

She shrugs. "Yeah."

"I wish you still would," he says, though not spitefully; he says it quietly, evenly, a simple truth, an earnest request.

But it still leaves a mark.

"You have to stop doing that," Clare says. "Stop being the romantic one."

Aidan looks surprised. "What?"

"It's not fair," she says. "I hate that you get to be the good guy here. It's not like I *want* to break up with you. It kills me just thinking about it, but I'm trying to be practical. Starting tomorrow, we're gonna be a million miles away from each other, and it doesn't make sense to do this any other way. So you have to stop."

"Stop...being romantic?" Aidan asks, looking amused.

"Yes."

"Have you ever thought that maybe you need to stop being so practical?"

Clare sighs. "One of us has to be."

"The one who planned a romantic scavenger hunt for our last night?" he says, looping an arm around her shoulders and giving her a little squeeze.

She rolls her eyes. "It's not a scavenger hunt."

"Well, whatever it is, I think it's suspiciously romantic for someone so annoyingly practical," he says, drawing her closer. Her head only comes up to his chest, so she has to tip her chin up to look at him. When she does, he leans down to kiss her, and even though they've kissed a thousand times before—have kissed, even, in this very parking lot—it still makes her stomach go wobbly, and she's seized by a sudden worry over how few of these they have left.

Together, they walk up the front steps of the school, and Clare tugs on the handle of the big wooden door, but it refuses to budge. She knocks a few times, in case there might be a security guard inside, but nobody answers.

"It's still a couple weeks till classes start," Aidan points out. "I'm sure nobody's here on a Friday night."

"I thought maybe there'd be summer school or something...."

"Let's just skip to whatever's next."

Clare shakes her head, not sure how to explain that this is the whole point of the night. To fit two whole years into one final evening; to dump all the pieces out of the box and then put them back together again in the right order so that they can see the whole thing spread out before them.

And so that they can say goodbye.

But to do that, they need to start at the beginning.

"No," she says, looking up at the stone building. "There has to be a way in. It's the first place we saw each other. . . ."

Aidan smiles. "Mr. Coady's Earth Science class."

"Exactly," she says. "Not that you remember."

"Of course I do."

"You do not. At least not that first day."

"Oh, come on," Aidan says, laughing. "How could anyone not remember *you*?"

"Impossible," she agrees, though she knows that's not true. Clare's been called a lot of things—smart and funny, driven and talented—but memorable certainly isn't one of them. The most important things about her—the ones she's most proud of—are apparent only once you get to know her. At first glance, she's almost entirely unremarkable: brown hair and brown eyes, average height and ordinary looks. Mostly, she just blends in, which has always been fine with her: You could do a lot worse in high school. But that meant that before Aidan, no boy had ever really noticed her before.

That first day, he'd sat down at the desk right behind hers. The teacher was handing out geodes to pass around the room, and when it was her turn with one of them, Clare cupped it in her hands. It looked like a regular old rock on the outside, but inside, it was full of glittering purple crystals. When she turned to pass it to the new kid, he kept his eyes on the stone. But later—after he'd finally noticed her, after they'd both realized that this was the start of something—she would come back to that moment again and again. Because that's how she felt when she was with him—like she'd been a rock her whole life, ordinary and dull, and it wasn't until she met him that something cracked open inside her, and just like that, she began to shine.

"We have to get inside," she says now, feeling oddly desperate.

Aidan gives her a strange look. "Does it really matter?"

"Yes," she says, rattling the door handle once more, though it's clearly useless. "We have to start this thing right."

She knows he doesn't understand why this is so important to her, and she's not sure she could tell him even if she tried. It's just that the clock is ticking down fast toward tomorrow, when everything will change. And this—this plan for their last night together—was supposed to be the one thing she could control.

All summer, Clare has been poring over class descriptions and campus maps and messages from her new roommate, trying to get a clearer picture of what her life will soon look like. But as much as she's read, as much as she's tried to find out, it's impossible to imagine the details. And it's the not knowing that's the hardest part.

There's so much of it, too. She doesn't know whether

she'll be able to balance Intro to Psychology with History of Japan, or whether she'll find someone to sit with in the dining hall during those first few crucial days, when loose collections of strangers start to solidify into groups of friends like hardening cement.

She doesn't know whether she'll get along with her roommate, a girl from New York City named Beatrice St. James, who seems to only want to talk about what bands she's been seeing this summer, and who—Clare suspects—will end up wallpapering their room with concert posters.

She doesn't know whether it's a mistake to leave her winter coat behind until Thanksgiving break, whether she'll find it unbearable to share a bathroom with twenty other people, whether girls from the East Coast will dress differently than the girls here in Chicago. She doesn't know whether she'll stand out or blend in, sink or swim, feel homesick or independent, happy or miserable.

And mostly, she doesn't know if she'll be able to survive all this without having Aidan on the other end of the phone.

Now she steps back from the wooden doors of the school with a defeated sigh.

"This," she admits, "is not a great start."

Aidan shrugs. "Who cares? I mean, don't you think this is close enough?"

"Close enough isn't good enough."

"Of *course* not," he says, rolling his eyes, but he follows her anyway as she makes her way along the building, past the staff parking lot and the auditorium and the whole east wing until they loop around to the back. Each time they pass another door, one of them jogs over to try it, but they're all locked, every single one of them.

Finally, just behind the school, they stand at the ground-floor window of Mr. Coady's classroom, their hands cupped against the glass as they peer inside. The room is dark and quiet, the chalkboard wiped clean, the black tables coated in a thin layer of dust, the rocks and other samples stacked neatly in cases along the opposite wall.

"It looks different," Aidan says. "Doesn't it?"

Beside him, Clare nods. "It almost seems like it's smaller or something."

"That must be because we're such big-time college students now," Aidan says with a grin, and they both step back again. He puts a hand on her shoulder. "I'm sorry we couldn't get inside."

She doesn't answer him; instead, she lifts her gaze to the top of the enormous window, then runs her fingers along the edges before rapping on the glass.

"I wonder if—" she begins, but Aidan cuts her off.

"No way," he says. "Don't even say it."

"I wonder if we could break in somehow," she says, ignoring him.

"Are you kidding?"

She blinks at him. "Not entirely."

"I don't think this is exactly the right time for either of us to get arrested," he says, the color rising in his cheeks, as it always does when he gets frustrated with her. "I have a feeling UCLA might frown upon that sort of thing, and I don't need to give my dad another excuse to be disappointed in me. Not when I'm just about out of here."

"Yeah, but—"

He holds up a hand, stopping her before she can continue. "I bet Dartmouth wouldn't be too thrilled about it, either," he reminds her, then gestures at the window. "Besides, we're right here. I realize the phrase 'close enough' isn't in your vocabulary, but why is this so important to you?"

"Because," she says, holding out the piece of paper, which is now balled up in her hand, "because this is our last night. And it's supposed to be perfect. And if we can't even get this right..."

Aidan's face softens. "This isn't a metaphor," he says. "If we don't check off everything on this list, all that means is we're flexible. We can roll with the punches. And that's a good thing, you know?"

"You're right," she says, swallowing hard. "I know you're right."

But still, she feels inexplicably sad. Because of course Aidan would think that. He wants desperately for everything to work out between them. If he walked over a patch of sidewalk right now that read CLARE AND AIDAN SHOULD ABSOLUTELY BREAK UP TONIGHT in brightly colored chalk, he'd still manage to somehow explain it away, to turn it around and make it into something positive.

Maybe the world isn't full of signs so much as it's full of people trying to use whatever evidence they can find to convince themselves of what they hope to be true.

For Clare, it seems pretty clear that a start like this doesn't bode well, and she feels a small glimmer of satisfaction at this: the prospect that she's been right all along, and that now, even the universe agrees that the only logical thing to do is part ways with Aidan.

But this is followed by a powerful wave of grief over the thought of actually having to do this, and she inches closer to him, feeling a little unsteady.

Aidan circles his arms around her automatically, and they stand there like that for a moment. In the distance, a car engine roars to life, and a few birds cry out overhead. Around them, the sky is fading from blue to gray, the edges going blurry, and Clare presses her cheek against the soft cotton of Aidan's shirt.

"Has anyone ever suggested that you might have some control issues?" he says with a smile, stepping back again. He takes the paper gently from her hand and smooths it out again. "Looks like this rules out number eight, too."

"The fall formal," she says with a nod. "Our first dance."

"Right," he says. "No chance of getting into the gym, either. Too bad I'm not allowed to be romantic, or else I'd make you dance with me right here."

"That's okay," she says. "I've already seen your moves."

"Not all of them. But don't worry. The night is still young. I'm saving my best stuff for later."

"I can't wait," she tells him, realizing just how much she means it.

Whatever happens later, they still have the rest of tonight.

And maybe that will be enough.

She links her arm with his, leaning into him as they start to walk back to the car. A breeze picks up, and for the first time Clare notices there's a bite to it: an early hint of autumn. Normally, she loves this time of year, and for weeks now, whenever she's told someone about Dartmouth, they've brought up the fall foliage in New Hampshire: the brilliant reds and yellows and oranges spread out over the campus and beyond. Clare has no doubt she'll find it enchanting once she gets there. But right now, she doesn't want to think about the coming of a new season. She just wants to live in this one for as long as she possibly can.

They're nearly to the car when she stops short.

"Shoot," she says, glancing back over her shoulder. "I meant to get a souvenir."

"So this *is* a scavenger hunt."

"I just thought it might be nice. You know, to have something from each place we stop tonight."

Aidan tilts his head at her. "You sure this wasn't just an elaborate plan to steal all those precious gemstones from the Earth Science classroom?"

"I think precious might be overstating it," she says. "But no."

"Okay, then," he says, stooping to grab an ordinary-looking rock from the ground at his feet. It's slate gray and rounded at the edges, and he rubs at it with the end of his plaid shirt before handing it over with a solemn look.

"Here," he says, and Clare feels the weight of it in her palm. She runs her thumb over the smooth surface, thinking back to that first day she'd seen him in class, the way his face had lit up when he turned over the rock to find all those purple crystals, like it was a fortune cookie or an Easter egg, the best kind of surprise.

"By my authority," Aidan is saying now, "as a B-plus student in Mr. Coady's junior year Earth Science class, I'm pleased to inform you that this little gem is now officially considered precious."

And here's the amazing thing: Now it was.

STOP #2

The Pizza Place

7:12 PM

For a while, the two of them stand just outside Slices, peering in through the fogged windows at all the unfamiliar faces.

"Didn't take them very long to move in, huh?" Aidan says, squinting at a corner booth that used to belong to some of his lacrosse buddies and that is now occupied by a cluster of sophomore girls all huddled over their phones.

"Out with the old..." Clare says lightly, though she feels a bit unsettled, too. After two weeks of goodbyes—two full weeks of sending their friends off one at a time—it feels like the town should be empty now. But here, it looks like any other night, the place completely packed, full of laughter and gossip and noise.

It's just that it's no longer *their* laughter and gossip and noise.

Aidan turns to face her, his blue eyes bright. "Let me guess," he says, rubbing his hands together. "First place I spilled something on you."

Clare shakes her head. "Nope."

"First place you saw me trip over my own feet? First time you saw me eat four slices of pizza in under ten minutes? First time I did that trick with a straw wrapper?"

"First place we talked," she says, stopping him, because she knows this could go on all night. "Not that it was much of a conversation, but it *was* the first time you spoke actual words to me."

"Oh, yeah," he says. "I remember now. I'm pretty sure I said you were the most beautiful girl I'd ever seen, and then asked you out right there on the spot."

"Close," Clare says with a smile. "You asked me to pass the Parmesan."

"Ah," he says. "One of my lesser-used pickup lines."

"Worked on me," she says as he pulls open the door.

Inside, the restaurant is thick with steam and filled with the smells of tomato and mozzarella. There's exactly one middle-aged couple in the far corner, hunched over their pizza and looking hassled by the chaos all around them. Otherwise, pretty much everyone is under the age of eighteen. That's the way it's been for as long as anyone can remember—this place isn't so much a restaurant as an off-campus lunch spot, an after-school meet-up point, a weekend hangout for the high school crowd. With its cracked leather booths and basic brown tables, the row of aging video games along one wall and the ironclad rule that slices come plain only, it's always sort of belonged to the town's younger population.

Just inside the doorway, Aidan stops short, and Clare

20

sees that their usual table is occupied by a few of the underclassmen from the lacrosse team. When they notice Aidan, they start to scramble to their feet, but he waves them back down again.

"Sorry," one of them says. He looks like a younger version of Aidan, round-faced and broad-shouldered and easygoing, but all the confidence drains right out of him at the sight of his former team captain. There's a note of awe in his voice as he apologizes. "We thought you'd already skipped town."

"Just about," Aidan says, clapping him on the back. "I'm headed out tomorrow."

"Do practices start right away?"

Aidan nods. "Preseason."

"Well, good luck, man," he says, and a few of the others chime in with well wishes, too. "Can't wait to hear all about it at Thanksgiving."

As they walk away from the table, Aidan takes Clare's hand, and she gives his a little squeeze. She catches sight of their reflection in the darkened window and realizes how lost they both look, like they've walked into a familiar room to find that all the furniture has been rearranged. But then they recognize a voice over near the register, and they both turn to see Scotty, leaning against the counter and scraping his pocket for coins.

Aidan steps up beside him, slapping down a five-dollar bill.

"It's on me," he says, reaching out to punch his friend's

shoulder, but it doesn't quite land because Scotty manages to dodge him, cuffing Aidan's ear before ducking away again. Clare hangs back as the two of them tussle the way they always do, circling each other like boxers until they notice Oscar—the hulking, largely silent cashier who has been there forever—watching them from behind the counter, looking entirely unamused.

"How many?" he asks, raising one eyebrow.

Aidan coughs, straightening up again. "Five," he says. "Please."

Oscar skulks off toward the oven without another word, and Scotty reaches over and gives Aidan's arm one last thump. "Thanks, man."

"I feel like I should start some sort of charity pizza fund for you before I go," he says. "I'm worried you'll starve without me."

"I'll manage," Scotty tells him, pushing up his thick-framed glasses. His dark eyes move between Aidan and Clare. "So," he says, "this is it, huh?"

Aidan nods. "Last night."

"For a little while, anyway," Scotty says.

Clare gives him a reassuring nod. "Just for a little while."

"And you two are, uh, doing okay?" he says, though it's clear what he's really asking is this: *Have you two decided what to do yet?*

"We're fine," Clare says, exchanging a look with Aidan.

"Who's fine?" Stella asks, appearing at their side. She's wearing all black, as usual, from her boots to her jeans to

22

her shirt and all the way up to her earrings, two feathery-looking things that get lost against her jet-black hair. She always manages to look as if she's preparing for a burglary, and Clare can't help feeling conspicuous next to her in spite of the fact that she's wearing a completely normal spectrum of colors: a blue sundress with a green cardigan.

"Where've you been?" Clare asks. "I thought you were coming over this afternoon."

"Oh," Stella says, twisting her mouth up at the corners. "Yeah. Sorry about that. I got caught up with something."

"With what?" she asks, but Stella's eyes have drifted over to Scotty, who is busy pouring oregano directly into his mouth. Most of it lands down the front of his Batman T-shirt, and he coughs and pounds on his chest, his eyes watering as he attempts to swallow the rest.

"It's like watching a toddler try to figure out how food works," Stella says, shaking her head. Scotty glares at her as he wipes the flakes from his shirt, and as always, Stella glares right back. She has a couple of inches on him in the staggeringly high heels she always insists on wearing, and after a moment, Scotty just shrugs and returns to the oregano.

The fact that the two of them have never gotten along usually isn't a problem. But with most of their friends off to school already, their crew has been whittled down to an awkward foursome: Scotty and Stella, already sniping over things that don't really matter, and Aidan and Clare, still at odds over all the many things that do.

Clare turns back to Stella. "You do realize I'm leaving tomorrow morning, right?"

"Uh, yeah," Stella says after a second. "And I'm leaving the next day."

"So where have you been?"

She frowns. "What do you mean?"

"Where've you been the last few days?" Clare repeats, ignoring Scotty and Aidan, who are looking back and forth between them as if watching a tennis match. At the moment, she doesn't care. All she wants is for Stella to snap out of whatever it is that's been going on with her lately. Because this is a big deal—leaving for college—and Clare could really use her best friend right now.

This is part of the job description, after all: the unspoken contract between all best friends. Clare is required to be there for Stella—to help her with college essays or tag along during endless thrift-shop excursions, to listen to her complain about the lack of interesting guys at their school, or her trio of exhausting younger brothers—and in return, Stella is supposed to be there for Clare, too. Even if it means giving her a hard time.

"You do know," she'd said once, earlier in the summer, interrupting one of Clare's frequent musings over what to do about Aidan, "that you're gonna break up with him eventually, right?"

They were in the car on their way to a movie, and Clare had flicked her eyes away from the road to meet Stella's, surprised. "Why do you say that?"

24

"Because," Stella said, propping a foot on the dashboard, "it's the truth. If it doesn't happen at the end of the summer, it'll happen a few weeks later, or at Thanksgiving, or Christmas, or next summer. It's inevitable."

"You don't know that."

"I do," Stella said, sounding maddeningly confident. "And meanwhile, you'll spend your whole freshman year sitting around watching your idiot roommate—"

"Beatrice," Clare said, exasperated. The moment she'd received her new roommate's contact information, Stella—who had herself requested a single room—immediately decided she didn't like the sound of her. And once they started texting, it only got worse. Stella insisted on scrutinizing every message that popped up on Clare's phone, rolling her eyes at the steady stream of band names and tour dates Beatrice was constantly mentioning.

"Fine," Stella said. "You'll be sitting around watching *your idiot roommate, Beatrice,* getting ready to go out to all those *totally dope* shows she likes so much while you're stuck back at the dorm in your flannel pajamas reading a book because you don't want to have any fun without Aidan, who—by the way—will be out in California getting convinced by *his* idiot roommate—"

"Rob."

"—his idiot roommate, Rob the surfer—"

"Rob the swimmer."

"Whatever," she said, clearly impatient. "Rob the swimmer, whose only concern is apparently whether Aidan is cool with getting a mini-fridge for their room, which I'm guessing is *not* so they can keep their veggies crisp. You know he'll definitely be dragging him out to meet girls. And even if he doesn't, Aidan will meet them anyway. Trust me. That's what college is all about."

"Aside from the whole learning thing."

"That's a very distant second," Stella said matter-of-factly. "The point is, do you really want to spend the next four years feeling guilty because you went out with your roommate one night and got all moony-eyed over some drummer with great hair and killer eyes?"

Clare laughed. "When have I ever gone moony-eyed over a drummer?"

"Well, you haven't," Stella admitted, giving her a sideways look. "But maybe that's just because you haven't let yourself imagine there are other possibilities out there."

"You mean besides Aidan."

"I mean," Stella said, "besides high school."

But all this was early in the summer, when Stella still cared enough to be honest. And when she had time to listen. Lately, she hasn't been around to do either, and even though they're both still here—at least for one more night—it sort of feels to Clare like her best friend has already left.

Maybe it's that Stella has been trying to give Clare and Aidan time to figure things out on their own, or maybe she's just been busy getting ready to leave herself. Or maybe it's that everything is coming to an end, and it's

26

easier to pretend it's not. Stella's never exactly been great at this sort of thing, anyway; she's allergic to sentiment and wary of emotion, so trying to get her to appreciate the significance of a milestone like this is a bit like trying to hug a skittish cat.

But still, after fourteen years of friendship, Clare refuses to let her slink off to college without some sort of meaningful goodbye.

Now Stella is leaning against the counter, absently pulling napkins from the dispenser, avoiding Clare's question. Finally, she shrugs.

"I don't know," she says. "I've been around."

"Not really," Clare says, shaking her head. "You haven't been returning calls, you've been showing up late—"

"Maybe she can't tell time," Scotty jokes.

"—you haven't been returning texts—"

"Or type," he chimes in again.

"Shut up, Scotty," they both say at the exact same time, and then they can't help themselves: As soon as their eyes meet, they start to laugh.

"I'm sorry," Stella says after a moment. "There's just been a lot going on. But we'll make up for it tonight. Really."

"You promise?" Clare asks, and Stella grins.

"I double-pinky promise," she says, holding out her fingers the way they used to do when they were kids. Clare smiles grudgingly, then hooks her pinkies around Stella's.

"Okay," she says as, behind them, Oscar thumps a fist

on the counter. They turn to see that their slices are ready. Aidan grabs the tray, and they all walk over to an empty table by the window.

As soon as they sit down, Scotty takes a huge bite of his pizza. The cheese is still steaming, and he winces, dropping it back onto his plate. "Too hot."

Stella rolls her eyes. "You're a numbskull."

"Word of the day?" Clare asks. Ever since taking the SATs, Stella has become obsessed with neglected vocabulary, picking a new word to work into conversation every day.

But she shakes her head. "Nope, that's just what he is. Today's word is *gobsmacked*, though I can't imagine I'll have a chance to use it, since there's never anything to be gobsmacked *about* around here." She glances over at Scotty with a grin. "Except maybe how much of a numbskull you are."

"Is that the kind of vocabulary that got you into a fine school like Florida State?" Scotty asks, picking at the crust of his pizza while he waits for the cheese to cool, and Stella—still a little sensitive about her only acceptance—gives him a withering look.

"Says the guy going to community college," she shoots back, and everyone goes abruptly still. Beside Clare, Aidan lowers his pizza, his mouth still half-open, and Stella, immediately realizing she's gone too far, turns pale.

For months now, this has been the one thing nobody has said. They've all spent the summer tap-dancing around the subject, and even now, on the eve of their departure, it feels somehow wrong to mention it.

Because of all of them, Scotty's the only one not going anywhere tomorrow.

Not that they didn't all have their share of rejection this past spring. As much as Stella's now looking forward to the warm weather in Florida, what she'd really wanted was to be closer to home, just downstate at the University of Illinois. Aidan hadn't gotten into Harvard, even as a legacy. And though Clare had been feeling confident about her chances at most of the places she'd applied, in the end, she'd gone only four for twelve.

Scotty, though, hadn't gotten a single yes. After a high school career spent coming up with ever more creative ways to escape his classes, it shouldn't have been a big surprise. But he and Aidan had spent so many months dreaming of conquering California together that it had taken Scotty weeks to get around to telling them, and when he finally did, they could all see how much it hurt. Since then he's done his best to make a joke of it—as he does with everything else—but Clare suspects that the only thing harder than leaving is being left behind.

His face is blank now, his ears pink at the tips, and his wiry frame is folded over the table in a way that makes him look even scrawnier than usual. Scotty's personality is normally big enough to make people forget about his size, but now it's like the air has gone right out of him.

Stella looks uncharacteristically earnest as she lays a

hand on his shoulder. "Hey," she says. "I'm sorry. You know I didn't mean—"

"Forget it," he says. "It's fine."

Clare is struck by a memory of Aidan, sometime just after they'd started dating, suggesting they set up Scotty and Stella. He was still new then, still clueless about the subtle dynamics of the eleventh-grade population, and still unaware of the fact that the two of them had been sparring—more or less uninterrupted—since kindergarten.

"But Scotty's so much fun," Aidan had said, which was true. Most of his other new friends were on the lacrosse team, but he'd met Scotty in art class, where they were the only two guys. Their first assignment had been to do a charcoal drawing of an object that was important to them. All the girls had sketched heart-shaped lockets and old clocks and ornate diaries. Aidan had drawn his lacrosse stick. But Scotty, of course, had come up with a Picasso-like rendering of a Mr. Potato Head, and when Aidan leaned over to compliment it without a hint of irony, they became instant friends.

"Yeah, but he's not right for Stella," Clare had told him. "Trust me. I've known them both a lot longer. They're oil and water."

But that wasn't exactly true. The problem wasn't that they *didn't* match; it was that they matched almost too well. They were both loud and funny, fearless and loyal, completely and utterly magnetic. It's just that they'd spent the better part of their lives repelling each other.

"Really," Stella is saying now, her hand still on his shoulder. She looks genuinely sorry. "That wasn't—"

"It's okay," Scotty says again, finally looking over at her. "I mean, it's what's happening, right? You guys are leaving and I'm staying here. It's not like ignoring it's gonna change anything."

Clare leans forward. "Yeah, but…"

"Really, I'm fine with it," Scotty says, and then his face cracks a little. "At least it means I won't have to share my pizza with you guys anymore."

"*Your* pizza?" Aidan asks, raising an eyebrow.

"Yeah," Scotty says with a nod, looking more cheerful already. "You guys'll be off eating your second-rate pizza in your totally untested new pizza places, and I'll still be here…with all this to myself."

Stella laughs, though Clare can tell it's more out of relief than anything else; she's just happy she didn't inadvertently tip the whole night off-balance. Scotty gives her a quick sideways glance before turning back to Aidan.

"And you know what the best part is?" he asks, his grin widening. "Once you finally hit the road, I'll be free and clear to ask a certain someone out. Maybe she can even come help me eat all that extra pizza…."

It takes a second for Scotty's meaning to register, but when it does, Aidan frowns. "Dude," he says, shaking his head. "This is the last time I'm gonna say it. You're not allowed anywhere *near* my sister."

This is a joke that only Scotty ever seems to find amusing. For Aidan, it's still a sore subject, and any reminder of last year's spring formal—when he and Clare had ducked out early to find his best friend kissing his younger sister in a darkened hallway—is enough to make the vein near his temple start to jump.

Aidan has always been protective of Riley, and even once the full story came out later—how her date had abandoned her, and Scotty had been nice enough to keep her company, and then one thing led to another—he was still furious. They didn't speak for weeks after that, Aidan and Scotty, in spite of Clare's attempts to patch things up between them. And though their friendship eventually recovered—helped along by Riley's admission that she was the one who kissed Scotty, and Scotty's frantic promises that it would never happen again—the subject is still a sensitive one for Aidan.

Most normal people would tiptoe around something like that, avoiding it like a conversational pothole. But not Scotty, who still insists on dredging it up from time to time, apparently hoping it will eventually get funnier. Which it hasn't.

"Too soon," Clare says, tossing a balled-up napkin at him. Across the table, Stella is flashing him a look that very plainly says: "Stop being an idiot."

Scotty's smile falters, and he gives them a shrug. "Okay,

okay," he says to Aidan, holding up his hands. "I was only kidding. I promise your sister is off-limits."

"Not like you'd have a chance anyway," Aidan says with a grunt, folding his arms across his chest.

"Hey," Scotty says, glancing up after an attempt to blow the wrapper off his straw fails completely. "I'm a catch."

This makes Stella laugh until she coughs. She pounds her chest a few times for effect, and Scotty's face clouds over again.

"What?" he says to Stella, a challenge in his voice. "Because you think I'm an idiot who couldn't get into any real colleges?"

"No," Stella says firmly. "Because I think you're an idiot with a big mouth and a thoroughly distorted sense of self-confidence."

As the two of them begin to bicker again, Clare glances over at Aidan, who is usually the referee in these situations. But at the moment, he's just watching them with an unreadable expression, his head tilted to one side. When she catches his eye, he gives her a weary smile, but in spite of everything, she can tell there's a part of him that's secretly enjoying it. This is just what he'd been hoping for tonight—something *normal*. Something light and silly and meaningless. Something that doesn't feel like an ending.

"I've got a brilliant idea," Clare says, and Scotty and Stella turn to her as if they'd forgotten anyone else was there. "Let's play the quiet game."

"I forfeit," Scotty says with a shrug, and Stella says, "Of

course you do," and just like that, they're off again on an unending circuit of teasing and arguing.

Clare leans back in her chair, looking around the tiny restaurant, where the light is warm and yellow. It would be impossible to count the number of nights that had begun or ended here, how many evenings had followed this very same pattern. She lets the blur of it all wash over her: the chirp of the video games and the girls singing tunelessly at a corner table, the smells of garlic and cheese, and the fluorescent lights of the sign in the darkened window, a red so electric it burns her eyes.

When she turns back again, Aidan is smiling at her.

"Hey," he says, leaning to bump her shoulder gently with his.

"Hey," she says quietly, so quietly it's almost lost in the noise of the place, a noise that no longer belongs to them. But Aidan hears her anyway.

"Any chance," he says, "that you could pass me the Parmesan?"

She reaches out for it, handing it to him with a little smile. But later, when nobody's looking, and the pizza is gone, and the shaker of cheese has been forgotten, she can't help herself: She picks it up again and slips it into her bag.

STOP #3

The Beach

7:54 PM

Outside the restaurant, the sky is now a deep pink, turning the trees and the lampposts and the pitched roof of the train station into silhouettes. Together, they wander over to Aidan's car, which is parked at an angle on the street, and then the four of them stand in a little semicircle around the hood, as they've done so many times before, waiting for someone to decide in what direction the night will go.

Usually, there are more of them, arguing about what should come next. But over the past couple of weeks, the rest of their friends have scattered across the country, setting out from their little suburb of Chicago in a dozen different directions like the spokes of a wheel: Caroline to Texas, Will to Ohio, and Elizabeth to North Carolina; Georgia left ages ago for a freshman-orientation wilderness trip in upstate New York, and the twins, Lucia and Mateo, had driven out to Stanford on their own, leaving time to see some sights along the way. Then, earlier this week, they'd lost most everyone else when the University of Illinois started up, dozens of their friends all migrating south at once.

"It's kind of weird, isn't it?" Clare asks, slipping her hands into her pockets.

Stella nods, her eyes fixed on the sidewalk. "And then there were four . . ." she says, and they all grow silent. Though dusk hasn't yet given way to dark, the streetlamps above them snap on, casting long shadows across the sidewalk.

Finally, Scotty clears his throat. "So what's the plan?"

"There's not much going on," Stella says, digging her phone out of her purse and scrolling through her texts. "Pretty much everyone's gone already. But apparently Andy Kimball's having people over later. And Mike Puchtler and those guys are going bowling. They said we could meet up, if we want."

"And if all else fails, we could always go hang out in my backyard," Scotty says. "Just for a change of pace."

"You have a backyard?" Clare asks in mock disbelief, since they ended up there pretty much every single night this summer, eating his mom's home-baked cookies beneath the starry sky as the clock wound down on another evening.

"Actually," Aidan says, thumping the hood of the car, and everyone turns to him, "I think we're gonna head out on our own."

Scotty's face falls, and he stares at his best friend. "So . . . this is it?"

"Yeah, what happened to quality time?" Stella asks,

frowning at Clare. "You're gonna leave me alone with this clown on our last night together?"

"No," Clare says quickly, over the sound of Scotty's protests. "Just for a little while. We still have some...talking to do. But we'll meet up with you guys later for sure."

"Right," Aidan says. "We just have to make a few stops first."

Stella laughs. "Let me guess: Clare made a list."

"Clare made a list," Aidan agrees with a grin.

"Pro and con?"

"More of a schedule for the evening, actually."

"Hey," Clare says, frowning at them. "How else are we supposed to figure this out?"

Scotty rolls his eyes. "Yeah, it's not like there's any way you could have seen this whole college thing coming. It must've really snuck up on you."

"It's not that," Clare says, glancing at Aidan, and when their eyes meet, he smiles almost without meaning to, which is the kind of smile she loves best: It's like a sneeze, a reflex, a twitch, helpless and automatic, and it only happens when he looks at her.

"It's more that we can't exactly seem to agree," he says, holding up his wrist to show them all his watch. "And I've only got, like, ten hours left to convince her. So no time to waste."

"But we'll call you later," Clare says as she gets into the car. When Stella gives her a skeptical look, she adds, "Double-pinky promise."

"You know who probably doesn't accept double-pinky promises?" Stella asks, walking over to rest her elbows on the open window. "Beatrice St. James."

Clare can't help laughing at this. "Which is why I'm so lucky to have *you*."

"You really are," she agrees. Then her face rearranges itself so that she looks more sincere than usual. She glances quickly behind her, then back at Clare. "Hey," she says, leaning in close, her voice a low whisper. "Good luck, okay? And listen..."

Clare tilts her head to one side, waiting.

"I know I might have said that I thought it would be crazy for you guys to try staying together..."

"Just once or twice."

"But," Stella continues, then pauses and licks her lips, "but...I don't know."

Clare stares at her. *I don't know* is not a phrase she usually associates with Stella, who is much more prone to statements like *I told you so* or *Trust me* or *Here's the plan.*

"I mean, what you guys have...it's pretty cool." She twists to look over her shoulder, to where Aidan and Scotty are talking a few feet away. "So, I don't know anymore. I guess...I guess I'm just saying that I have no idea what you should do."

"That's very helpful," Clare says, patting her hand. "Thanks for the pep talk."

In spite of herself, Stella laughs. "Sorry."

"No, it's fine. It's great, actually. I've missed getting to talk to you about this stuff lately, especially since it's been so hard to figure out—"

Behind Clare, the driver's-side door is flung open, and Aidan drops into the other seat, looking over at both of them with an expectant smile.

"Ready?" he asks, and Clare gives him a startled nod.

"We'll see you guys later," Stella says, tapping the car door once before stepping back to stand beside Scotty, who lifts a hand.

"Yeah," he says cheerfully. "Hopefully you'll still be speaking to each other by then."

Clare waves back, but the words send a little jolt through her. She realizes that he's right. The next time she sees them, there's a pretty good chance that she and Aidan will have broken up, and everything will be different.

"You ready?" Aidan asks, turning the key in the ignition.

Clare looks out through the dirty windshield, watching as Stella and Scotty walk off together, and then she nods. "Ready."

As they drive, the headlights cut through the bluish dusk, sweeping across the town square and the train station, the library, and the park with its statue of a deer, stoic beneath a coat of blue graffiti.

Aidan is sitting low in the seat, one hand on the wheel, the other twisting the dial of the radio. He doesn't have to ask the reason behind the next stop. They've been there together so many times that the drive feels almost mechanical, as if they're not so much steering as being pulled in the direction of the beach.

Clare plays with the edge of her seat belt, where the fabric is frayed, twisting a loose thread around her finger. She can't stop thinking about what Scotty said. For years, she's been planning every aspect of her life—college essays and applications, extracurricular activities and sports, volunteering and homework—with an eye toward leaving for college. Yet somehow, she hadn't managed to prepare herself for leaving *Aidan*, which feels so much bigger than the rest of it.

They've known for months that they'll have to part ways tomorrow. No matter what they decide about the future—stay together or break up—it doesn't change that. At six thirty tomorrow morning, Clare will start the long drive to New Hampshire with her parents, and just a few hours later, Aidan will be on a flight to California.

But now that it's so close, she realizes just how deeply she's misjudged the distance; for a long time, it had felt like something way out on the horizon, this moment, something she had to squint to make out, so far away it didn't seem quite real. Until now, when it's suddenly hurtling toward them at an impossible pace, so swiftly that it doesn't matter whether or not Clare is ready for it. There's no preparing at this point. There's only steeling yourself. There's only hoping for the best.

She leans back against the seat, letting her head roll

to the side. "I wish you were driving me," she says, and Aidan glances over at her. The radio has landed on a bluegrass station, and the sound of a guitar rises and swells in the otherwise quiet car.

"Isn't that what we're doing?"

"No, I mean tomorrow. It would give us more time...."

"Well, much as I'd love to whisk you away, I'm sure your parents would be disappointed not to take you." He smiles, but there's something hard in the line of his jaw. "I hear this is kind of a big milestone."

Clare reaches over and rests a hand on his shoulder. "I'm sure yours would take you if you just asked," she says, though she's actually not certain that's true. His parents had been crushed that he hadn't gotten into Harvard, especially his father. He'd been the first one in his family to go to college, and for a poor kid from south Boston, getting a full scholarship to Harvard had been like going to the moon. He spoke of it constantly with the kind of reverence usually reserved for church. To him, it was a magical place, one that had opened every door of opportunity for him, and it was his greatest wish that his son follow in his footsteps.

Aidan, on the other hand, was nothing but relieved by the rejection. He'd never had any interest in Harvard, with its cloistered buildings and hallowed halls and snow-covered paths; there was too much history there, too many expectations. He'd always wanted a place with sunshine and parties and cheering stadiums, a school that was thrumming with life and activity, somewhere big enough for him to make his own memories.

After a recruiting trip last fall, where he met with the Harvard lacrosse coach and took a tour of the campus, Aidan had returned even more set against it.

"You should've seen my dad," he'd told Clare when he got back. "He had this goofy smile on his face the whole time. And when we went to watch a practice? It was insane. He's never asked me a single thing about lacrosse, not ever, and then all of a sudden, the way he was talking to the coach, you'd think he was a lifelong fan."

"Yeah, but what did *you* think?" Clare had asked.

Aidan shrugged. "It's not for me."

"How do you know?"

"I just know," he said simply. "How do you know you want a small liberal arts school?"

Clare shook her head. "I just do."

"Exactly."

She knew he was right. There was a certain amount of gut involved in this decision to launch yourself into some random part of the world, blindly charging headlong into an entirely new life. She'd always known she was bound for the East Coast in the same way Aidan had always been headed west: instinctively and without logic.

But his father had never wanted to hear it, and when Aidan hadn't gotten into Harvard, he couldn't hide his disappointment. He'd always figured his son would come around to the idea of it. But really, he should have been worrying that Harvard would come around to the idea of Aidan.

There was no real reason why he shouldn't have been accepted: His grades weren't spectacular, but they were surprisingly good, given his lack of effort, and he was a legacy, not to mention a highly sought-after lacrosse player.

Still, he hadn't gotten in.

Which was more than okay with Aidan.

But he knows all too well that if he were headed to Cambridge tomorrow, there's no doubt his parents would be driving him there, giddy and excited. Instead, he's going to the school of *his* dreams. But he's doing it all alone.

When he shrugs, Clare's hand slips off his shoulder.

"You know it was always Harvard or bust with them," he tells her.

"Well, maybe it'll be better to say goodbye at the airport anyway," she says, her voice a little too bright. "You'd probably look a lot less tough if you showed up to the first day of practice with your parents."

"Come on," he says, relaxing his stiff-armed grip on the wheel and flashing her a little grin. "I'd look tough holding a *teddy bear.*"

She can't help laughing at this. He looks so earnest right now, his freckles lost in the dark, his eyes big. With his red hair and round face, his lanky, too-tall frame, he always seems to Clare a bit like a teddy bear himself. So it's sometimes disconcerting when she watches him on the field, dodging and checking, twisting and attacking, sprinting to beat defenders to the goal. It's beautiful, in a way, seeing him like that, powerful and agile and surprisingly quick. But she's always a little relieved when he removes his helmet at the end of the game, and he's just Aidan again, pink-cheeked and sweaty and happy to see her.

"You'd look tough even if you had *two* teddy bears," she assures him, giving his arm a little pat.

As they near the lake, the houses start to get bigger, sprawling mansions set back on enormous lawns. It's such a far cry from their end of town—where the lots are the size of postage stamps, and the houses sit shoulder to shoulder—that it almost feels like they've traveled from somewhere a lot farther away.

With her window rolled down, Clare can already hear the rush of waves from the beach below. Aidan turns onto the drive that leads down to the lake, a winding road that cuts a path along a ravine, and when they reach the bottom, there's nothing but the water and the sand and a narrow strip of parking lot dotted with a few scattered cars.

They park and walk out along a stone path, moving away from the pavilion with the picnic tables and grills, and the playground, which stands quiet now in the dusk, and out toward where the length of sand is wider and a little bit rougher. The sky is streaked with orange, bright against the violet backdrop, and the water is golden in the last of the light. Clare's breath hitches in her throat at the sight of it.

"I'm going to miss this," she says as she slips off her

sandals. Beside her, Aidan is kicking off his sneakers, so that they go arcing out onto the beach. They step off the path, their bare feet sinking into the sand, to collect them again.

"I'll still be pretty close to the water, I think," he says as they begin to walk toward one of the enormous piles of boulders that act as breakers against the waves, jutting out over the lake in regular intervals along the coast.

"You *think*?" she says, staring at him. "Haven't you looked at a map?"

Aidan shrugs. "I figured it would be better if it's all a surprise."

"*All?* Have you even read any of your orientation stuff?"

"I looked at some of the lacrosse packet," he says, and before she can reply, he gives her a hard look. "You sound like my parents."

"Unfair," she says, stopping abruptly.

He slings an arm around her shoulders, drawing her close, and they half stumble forward again in the soft sand. "Sorry," he whispers, his mouth close to her ear. "I'm just…"

"I know," she says, circling an arm around his waist.

They climb the rocks together, stepping carefully where the waves have made the surfaces dark and slick, and once they've reached their spot, they sit together with their feet dangling off the edge.

Far out in the water, they can see the winking light of the tall yellow weather buoy, which was put in a couple of years ago to send environmental data back to a lab somewhere in Indiana. With its broad base and skinny top, and the sensors that appear more like googly eyes than anything else, it looks to all the world like a drowning robot, and they've grown rather fond of it over the years, dubbing it Rusty after a lively discussion about the effect of salt water on metal.

Worrying over Rusty's well-being has become one of their favorite pastimes, and last summer Scotty suggested that someone should swim out and give the poor guy a life jacket or an inner tube or something. A few of them made a halfhearted attempt, but the buoy was a pretty long way from the shore, and nobody was quite committed enough to the joke to go the full distance. Still, every time they went down there, someone inevitably brought it up again, and the challenge was passed around once more as they wondered who would finally save poor Rusty.

Now Aidan squints out at the buoy, which flashes white against the pale line of the horizon. "Guess he'll have to live without us for a little while."

"I have a feeling he'll make it."

Aidan turns to look at her. "I think this is my favorite stop yet."

"That's just because it's the first one you actually remember," she points out, and he laughs.

"True," he says, scooting closer. "But I'm in it more for the reenactment."

"You can't replicate a first kiss," Clare tells him, glancing back over her shoulder to where everything had started that night, the night of the bonfire. It wasn't any sort of special occasion, just a small party, a spontaneous gathering of friends and acquaintances, with a blazing fire at the center of it all that threw off sparks in the night and made everything hazy and indistinct.

Clare had lost Stella only moments after arriving, so she'd wandered over to the cooler on her own, but once she got there, she hesitated. It was a bitter autumn night, teetering on the edge of winter, and the heat from the fire wasn't enough to warm her all the way through. She was still standing there, trying to decide whether or not she actually wanted a cold drink, when Aidan stepped up and plunged a bare hand into all the ice, fishing around for a can and then handing it to her with a gallant smile.

"Thanks," she'd said, holding the can between her blue mittens. "Though if you're gonna play bartender, you really need some gloves."

He glanced down at his hand, which was raw and red and still dripping, and then, without thinking, without even realizing what she was doing until it was done, Clare had reached out and cupped his hand between her own.

Their eyes met for a startled moment, and then he smiled.

"Much better," he said. "Thanks."

After that, they'd started talking—about what? She can't even remember now—and soon they were walking down toward the water together, daring each other to stick a toe in, though it was much too cold.

"Isn't it kind of cool that there's all this sand, but each grain is totally different?"

Aidan gave her a funny look. "Guess I must not have been paying attention that day."

"What day?"

"In Earth Science," he said. "I have a habit of daydreaming."

"Oh," she said, shaking her head. "No, I actually read that somewhere else." She stopped walking and lifted a finger, pointing up at the sky. "I also read that there are even more stars than there are grains of sand in the whole world. Isn't that crazy?"

He was looking down at her with a mystified expression, and Clare bit her lip, feeling a little self-conscious. She'd spent enough time watching Aidan over the last few weeks to know that a guy like him probably wouldn't go for a girl who read science magazines in her spare time, and the wheels in her head spun frantically in an effort to find some other topic of conversation, something he'd be more interested in.

But then he bent down and scooped up a handful of sand, sifting through it with his thumb. She could see his lips moving, see that he was murmuring under his breath as he stared at the grains in his palm. After a little while, he looked up again.

"That *is* pretty crazy," he said, and she felt a wave of relief.

"Right?"

He cupped his hand, then tipped it to one side, letting the sand pour back out onto the beach. "There's got to be, like, thousands just right there. And that's only one handful. From one beach. In one town. In one state. In one country. That means there must be about a zillion stars." He tilted his head back to take in the speckled sky with wide eyes, then laughed. "I mean...wow."

"Yeah," Clare said, unable to keep from smiling as she watched him. "Wow."

Eventually, they clambered up onto the rocks, continuing to talk until it was late—too late—and the fire behind them had died out, and everyone else had drifted back to their cars. Being there with him, it felt like no time at all had passed, but at some point, Clare heard her name shouted from a distance, the words made thin by the chilly breeze. She half turned in that direction, but just as she was about to get up, just before she could leave, Aidan leaned over and kissed her, and the surprise of it was enough to warm her straight down through her toes.

Even hours later—after he walked her back to the car and she finally let go of his hand, after she told Stella on the ride home what had happened, after she crawled into bed and lay there staring at the ceiling, reliving the whole night again—she felt all lit up inside. Some unseen part of her, which had only ever been lukewarm, was suddenly blazing.

She smiles at him now, still half-caught in the memory.

"It was perfect," she says. "Nothing will ever come close."

"Nothing?" Aidan says with mock horror. "You're telling me that none of the thousands of other kisses we've had over the last couple of years have compared? I mean, if I'd known that, I wouldn't have been trying so hard."

She gives his chest a little shove. "You weren't trying *that* hard."

"Hey, that was some of my best stuff," he says. "Remember that time we made out in the coat closet at Andy's party? Or that night in the park?" He pauses for a second, and then his face brightens. "Or that kiss we had in your basement?"

"Which—"

He cuts her off with a grin. "You know which one."

"Oh," Clare says, blushing a little. "Right."

"So you're saying none of those were better?"

"They were all great. They just weren't the first. Firsts are always the ones that last. You know?"

Without warning, he brings his face to hers, but when their lips meet, there's too much momentum behind it, their depth perception lost in the gathering dark. He cups the side of her face with his hand—the way they do in the movies—which is something he's never done before, not once in all the time they've been dating, making the whole thing feel off somehow, theatrical and staged and too full of effort.

When she pulls back a bit too abruptly, he looks wounded. "What?"

"Nothing," she says. "It's just—I think you're trying too hard to make it special."

"I thought that was the point of all this," he says, his voice resigned. "I thought we were supposed to be reliving all the big moments."

"We are," she says. "But we've got to talk about the future, too."

He doesn't respond to this, only shifts away from her a little so that he's fully facing the water. Ahead of them, the sky is still painted orange at the very edge, while heavier clouds are gathering at their backs, bringing with them the smell of rain.

"Look," Clare says finally, after a few minutes have passed in silence. "You know how I feel about you...." When he doesn't respond, she clears her throat, more insistent this time. "Aidan. You know that, right?"

He nods, his jaw set.

"But I just... I think we might have an expiration date." The waver in her voice surprises her; it's not the first time she's said this, but still, it hovers between them, clattering and definitive. "And we need to talk about it."

"Can't we wait just a little longer?"

"We can't keep putting it off."

"I bet we could," he says with a hint of a smile. "I'm really, really good at putting things off."

She smiles, too. "That's true."

"How about this?" he says, turning to her, his eyes hopeful. "Let's pretend—"

"Aidan."

"No, hear me out. Let's pretend—just for a few minutes— that we're both going to the same place tomorrow."

"Yeah?" she says, and he tucks her under his arm, resting his chin against the top of her head, so when he talks, she can feel the vibration of it, low and gravelly.

"Yeah," he says. "The way I see it, we'll meet up every morning and go to the dining hall together, and we'll eat awful bacon and cold eggs and catch up on our work. Then we'll walk to class—you to some Advanced Theory of Something-or-Other and me to Intro to Beginner's Goofing-Off-for-Jocks—and then afterward, we'll hang out on the quad, and I'll be playing guitar—"

"You're tone-deaf," she points out, and he shrugs.

"Yeah, but we're just pretending, and that's what everyone does on a quad."

"Okay, what else?"

"We'll go to the library together every night, and you'll study while I throw little balled-up pieces of paper at you and mix up all your color-coded sticky notes."

"I don't have—"

He leans to give her a stern look. "Yes, you do. You totally have color-coded sticky notes. And highlighters, too."

She rolls her eyes. "Fine."

"And we'll eat ramen noodles for dinner and sneak into the bars together and go to boring lectures and watch a million movies on Sunday afternoons. And we'll have roommates who are never there, so we can sleep over every night, all cozy on those tiny dorm room beds, and we'll wake up every single morning just like this," he says, tightening his arms around her. "All tangled up together."

Clare closes her eyes. "Why..." she begins, then trails off, her voice unexpectedly full of emotion. "Why didn't we just decide to do that?"

"Because we agreed that we have to live our own lives," he says a little sadly. "And I get that. I do. But it doesn't mean we can't still be together."

"Yeah, it does," she says, sitting up a little, feeling like she's just awoken from a deep sleep. She swivels around so that they're facing each other. "'Cause that's the thing— we won't actually *be together*. We're going to have three thousand miles between us."

"Right, but—"

She shakes her head. "And it's more than just the distance," she tells him. "You know it is. Nobody survives this kind of thing. You pretend it's going to work, and you make all these promises, and then you talk on the phone every night and text each other between classes and maybe manage a visit during fall break or something. But then everything's awkward, because so much has changed, and you don't fit into each other's lives anymore. And then the cute guy from down the hall shows up to say hi, and even though he's just a friend, you get jealous, and we get into a fight, and then you take off, and I leave you a million voice mails, and send you a thousand long and wordy e-mails, but you're still bitter, so you go hook up with some random girl, which I hear about somehow, because let's be honest, you always hear about these things somehow, and then I'm furious, because me and the cute guy were only friends, but what you did was unforgivable, and so it's over, just like that, and then we have to see each other at Thanksgiving, at some party or at the bowling alley or even at Scotty's house, and you end up standing in the corner looking all forlorn, and I'm stuck whispering to Stella in the other corner, and worse than that, there's just all this stuff between us, jealousy and resentment and bitterness, and it's awful, because there used to be nothing between us, and not in a bad way, but in the best way, because we never had any space for that kind of stuff, but now it's there, and there's no changing that, and the whole thing just ends up being sad and awkward and inevitable and totally, horribly, completely heartbreaking. And who wants that?"

Aidan stares at her for a long time. "Not me," he says eventually, looking a little bit stunned.

"Exactly," Clare says, satisfied.

"So...why don't you just avoid the cute guy to begin with?"

"That's not the point," she says, though she can tell he's only teasing her. "Wouldn't you rather end things now, on our own terms, so we can at least still be friends?"

"I don't want to be friends."

"That's all we'd be anyway, from that far away."

He shakes his head. "That's what you think?"

"I guess so."

"God, Clare," he says, his face darkening. "I hate how everything always has to be so black-and-white with you. Just because we wouldn't get to . . . I mean, it's not like we'd only be pen pals or anything."

"I know, but—"

"This kind of thing doesn't come along that often," he says, his eyes flashing now. "And you want to just throw it away because it might get too hard. Or because you want to be free to meet someone new."

"It's not that," she tells him, trying to keep the frustration out of her voice. "It's just . . . we're so young. It's not *that* crazy to think we might not end up with the person we dated in high school."

Aidan gives her a sour look. "We're not your parents," he says, picking up a small stone and tossing it out over the water, where it disappears into the gray chop of the waves. "This isn't the same thing."

Clare's mom and dad had both been married before, each to their high school sweetheart. It wasn't until after those other marriages had fizzled, after they'd both gotten divorced, that they were lucky enough to find each other.

To Clare, it seems like there must be a lesson in there somewhere.

"You don't know that," she says with a frown.

"I do, actually," Aidan says, chucking another rock out into the lake, more forcefully this time. "Because they're just one example. There are a million other couples who met in high school who are probably still ridiculously happy. You just refuse to see that, because you've already made up your mind."

Clare gives him a wounded look. "That's not fair."

"Isn't it?" Aidan says without meeting her eyes. "It's like that time we carried that table down to the basement for your parents. We both had it, and it was going fine. And then you dropped your side of it, and the whole thing turned into this huge mess, with the drywall and the broken leaf and my shoulder—"

"I get it," Clare says, stopping him short. "You think I'm giving up on this. But I'm not. I'm just trying to save us the trouble."

"Well, maybe I don't want to be saved," he says, finally looking at her. "Maybe I believe in this enough for both of us."

"You can't wish this into working," she says, feeling miserable even as she does. She can see the anger draining out of Aidan, his eyes going distant, and she wants to take it all back, to say something reassuring, to give him some thread of hope. But it's too late for that. It wouldn't be fair to either of them. Instead, she reaches for his hand, but he pulls it away, and she sighs. "I'm sorry, but believing isn't enough."

Aidan stares out over the water, his forehead crinkled. "How do you know unless you've tried?"

"I just know," Clare says quietly. "I just have this feeling."

"Well," Aidan says, "so do I."

She waits for him to say more, but he doesn't. He lets out a long breath, running a hand over the top of his head, where his hair used to stick up in a way that Clare always found oddly charming, and her heart seizes at even this smallest of changes: his new college haircut. It's hard not to think about how many more are still to come.

"I think I liked it better when we were avoiding talking about all this," he says eventually, and Clare nods.

"Me too," she admits. "But we have to figure it out. The clock is ticking."

"You make it sound like a bomb," he says. "You make *us* sound like a bomb."

"Maybe we are."

There's nothing either of them can say to that; they don't even bother to try. Instead, they look out toward the horizon, the last streaks of pink and the first few visible stars and the drowning robot, forever destined to flail hopelessly in the darkening water. Clare pulls her knees up to her chest, shivering a little, though she doesn't feel cold.

After a moment, Aidan leans forward and picks up another small stone. "Your souvenir," he says quietly as he hands it over to her.

"My collection," she says, slipping it into her bag, "is gonna get pretty heavy."

"I'll help you carry it."

"You won't be there," she tells him, blinking fast, willing herself not to cry.

"I will for now," he says, reaching into her bag and taking out both rocks, then raising his eyebrows when he feels the Parmesan shaker. As he lifts it, some of the flakes go floating off in the breeze, and for a second it almost looks like snow.

"Okay," she agrees. "For now."

"For now," he repeats, as if getting used to the sound of it, and then he leans forward to kiss her again, and this time there's nothing showy about it; this time it's just right: sad and sweet and heartbreakingly familiar.

"Much better," she says, cupping his hands in hers.

STOP #4

The Gallaghers' House

8:40 PM

They're nearly back to the car when Aidan pauses to fish his phone out of his back pocket. He stands for a moment in the middle of the parking lot, his face lit by the bluish light of the screen, before looking up at Clare with a sigh.

"I don't suppose my house was on the list, was it?"

"Not other than meeting you there," she says as they reach the car. "But we can definitely stop by again. I should probably say goodbye to your parents, anyway. How come?"

"Riley needs a ride to the bowling alley," he says, leaning against the trunk. There's a Harvard sticker on the bumper that's peeling at the corner, and he chips at it with the heel of his sneaker.

"That's totally fine," she says. "Bowling is on the list anyhow."

"Next?"

"No, but we can switch around the order. I mean, it doesn't *really* matter, right?"

He smiles. "Look at you, being so flexible."

"That's me," she says, bending down to brush the sand from her legs, and then opening the passenger-side door. "Rolling with the punches. Come what may. Easy breezy."

"Oh, yeah," he says, grinning at her over the top of the car. "Super breezy."

By the time they turn onto Aidan's street, it's fully dark, and as usual, the whole block is already lit up, the windows blazing. When he pulls into the driveway, they sit there for a minute, the engine still ticking, and then he turns to Clare with a weary smile.

"Let's make this really quick, okay?"

She nods. "Hi and bye."

"I like that," he says. "Hi and bye. Quick and painless."

As they walk up the stone path that leads to the side door, Clare remembers the first time she ever came over. It was just before Christmas, and she'd assumed the giant gold cross and elaborate nativity scene set up on a table in the foyer were seasonal decorations. She'd been wrong. As it turned out, they lived there all year, alongside an impressive collection of cross-stitched prayers in delicate frames and pillows with Irish blessings and shamrocks all over them.

"May the road rise to meet you..." she'd whispered as she read one of them on that first visit, standing in the front hallway with Aidan, the smells of Mrs. Gallagher's pot roast drifting in from the kitchen.

"And the wind be always at your back," he finished,

stepping up beside her. "Except when my mother is cooking, in which case you have to hope the wind shifts somewhere else entirely."

They'd only been together a month or so at that point, and she'd been caught off guard by the feel of the place, so crowded and close, and so different from Aidan, who was clumsy and loud, far too big for a house so cluttered.

Even then, he seemed ready to break free.

Now, as they near the side door, they can hear a swell of voices from inside. Clare glances at Aidan, but it's impossible to tell what he's thinking. Above them, a cluster of light-drunk bugs make pinging noises as they bump up against the glass bulb, and a car rushes past on the quiet street, a few people whooping out the window.

"If you hadn't put so much pressure on him..." Aidan's mother is saying from inside, her voice rising in a way Clare has never heard before. There's a clatter of something metal being set down hard, and then footsteps moving across the kitchen, which is just on the other side of the door.

"And you don't care that he lied to us?" his dad shouts back. Clare looks at Aidan with alarm, but his eyes are fixed on the straw mat at their feet, the words CEAD MILE FAILTE stamped across it: A HUNDRED THOUSAND WELCOMES in Gaelic.

Usually, that's the way it feels here. His parents might be a little intense, but they're also generally friendly and polite. They have high expectations for their kids, and their house rules are a lot stricter than at Clare's (whose parents are so trusting that she's sometimes relieved she doesn't have a sibling, on the off chance the kid wouldn't have turned out to be as responsible as she is). But the Gallaghers have always been more than welcoming, offering drinks and snacks, making room at the table, asking about her classes whenever Clare comes over—which isn't very often, since Aidan usually insists they go to her house.

"Your parents play music and make tacos and tell jokes and watch shows other than the news," Aidan explained when she asked why they didn't go to his place more often. They'd been dating about six months at that point—which felt like a lifetime to Clare—yet she'd been to his house only a handful of times. "Besides," he'd continued, "your parents actually like you. And me."

"Your parents like you," Clare had said uneasily, but Aidan only shook his head.

"Do you know what my dad does? He trades in futures."

"I don't even know what that means."

"It's a stock thing. I don't really know, either. But it's kind of ironic, right? All he cares about is my future. He doesn't care about who I am now. All he wants for me is Harvard and grad school and a big job with a suit and tie."

"Maybe that just means he cares enough to—"

"No," Aidan said, cutting her off. "All it means is that he's used to betting big. But he doesn't realize I'm a bad bet."

"You don't know—"

"Yeah," he said, "I do. Trust me, I know. I don't want any of that stuff. I wish he'd just realize I'm a lost cause already and move on to Riley. She actually *wants* to go to Harvard. That pretty much makes her the automatic favorite in the Gallagher household."

"Come on," Clare said. "You know he loves you both."

"I don't know about that. He definitely likes the idea of me. And he likes my potential. But I don't think he actually likes *me* all that much."

Clare wasn't sure what to say to that. "What about your mom?"

"Well, she works in an antiques shop," he said. "So if we're sticking with the whole futures analogy, that probably means she liked me better when I was little."

"You were probably a lot less trouble then."

He flashed her a grin. "I've always been trouble, baby."

Clare couldn't help laughing. "You know, if you spent some more time over there, maybe they'd get to know the actual, present-tense you a little better."

But Aidan just smiled. "I think I'd rather spend more time here with the actual, present-tense *you*."

Now, as they stand listening at the door, Clare glances down at the words on the mat again, feeling like they must be at least a few thousand welcomes short at the moment.

"That's not the point," Mrs. Gallagher is saying from inside, and to Clare's surprise, Mr. Gallagher roars back at her: "Of *course* it's the point!"

Aidan leans back from the door, lifting his eyes to meet

63

Clare's. "Still feeling breezy?" he asks with a grim smile, and then, before she can ask what they're talking about, before she can figure out what's going on, he turns the knob and pushes open the door.

As soon as he does, his parents both fall abruptly silent, whirling to face them. Mr. Gallagher—an even taller, thicker version of his son—is red-faced, his hands balled into fists. And beside him, Mrs. Gallagher—small and slight and as freckled as her kids—stares at them with glassy eyes.

"Hi, Clare," she says, a little breathless. "It's nice to see you, sweetie."

"Hi," Clare says, searching for something to follow this. "We just…" She trails off, hoping for Aidan to fill the space, but he's just standing there beside her with his head bent, his hands shoved into the pockets of his jeans. Nobody says anything, and Clare looks around at each of them in turn, completely lost.

"Aidan," Mr. Gallagher says eventually, rubbing his forehead wearily with the heel of his hand. "I think we need a couple of minutes."

Clare is so busy trying to work out what's going on—the mysterious undercurrent of anger in the room and the feeling that everyone else knows something she doesn't—that it takes a second for the words to register. When they do, she glances once at Aidan, who gives a little nod without meeting her eyes, then lifts her hand in an awkward wave to his parents.

"Sure, yeah," she says, overly agreeable. "I'll just go up and let Riley know we're here."

She hurries through the open door of the kitchen without a backward glance, then out into the front hallway, where she lingers for a minute, tempted to stay and listen. But the voices from the next room are low and hard to make out, and there's a painting of St. Patrick gazing down at her with disapproval, so she turns to head up the stairs, taking them two at a time.

At the top, she pauses in front of Aidan's room out of habit, taking in the familiar terrain: the piles of dirty clothes and the unmade bed, the teetering stacks of books and the collection of lacrosse sticks leaning like brooms in the corner. One of his Chicago Cubs T-shirts is twisted in a lump on the floor at her feet, and she stoops down to pick it up, burying her face in it, memorizing the smell of him, missing him already, though he's just downstairs. She thinks about taking it with her, another souvenir for her collection, but she knows it's one of his favorites, so instead, she folds it neatly and lays it gently on the edge of his bed, then continues down the hall to Riley's room.

"Come in," Riley calls when Clare knocks, and she peeks her head around the door to find the younger girl sprawled out on her bed with a well-worn copy of the sixth Harry Potter book. She has the same auburn hair as her brother, but it's long, even longer than Clare's, and her red-framed glasses make her face look very thin. She's only two years behind them in school, but she's so slight and willowy, so sweet and enthusiastic, that she often seems much younger than that.

"Hey," she says, scrambling up when she sees that it's Clare. "Sorry, I didn't realize you guys would be here so soon." She grabs a gray corduroy bag from the floor and starts throwing things into it. "I'll be ready in a minute, I swear."

"It's okay," Clare says, closing the door behind her. "I think we've got some time, actually."

Riley stops what she's doing and looks up. "Oh," she says, her face growing serious. "Yeah. I guess we probably do, huh?" She sits down.

Clare takes a seat on the edge of her bed, which is covered in an old purple quilt. "Do you know what's going on?" she asks. "They seem really mad. It can't still be about UCLA, can it?"

"Sort of," Riley says, then changes her mind and shakes her head. "Well, no, actually. Not really. I mean…it's about Harvard."

Clare frowns at her, surprised. All talk of Harvard—which had once been a constant source of conversation around the Gallagher house—seemed to have died out after Aidan's rejection. Not long after he'd broken the news to his father—who'd been stunned into a restless, disappointed silence that had stretched out for days—Aidan had gotten his acceptance to UCLA and a few other schools on the West Coast. And so, it had seemed, there was nothing left to discuss.

"He must be at least a little bit happy for you, right?" Clare had asked Aidan at the time. Her own parents—who were the greatest of cheerleaders, supportive to an extent that was sometimes a little suffocating—would have been encouraging even if Clare had announced she was dropping out of school altogether. So it was sometimes hard for her to understand Mr. Gallagher, with his lofty expectations for his son, who had—in spite of getting rejected from Harvard—been accepted to three other very good universities. And yet he still couldn't seem to muster the appropriate level of enthusiasm. "UCLA's such a great school. And the lacrosse team—"

"He doesn't care about lacrosse," Aidan had said, giving her an impatient look, though nothing could hide the joy in his eyes whenever the subject of UCLA came up. He was practically giddy at the thought of it, and there was a new lightness to him—a dizzy, expansive relief—that Clare couldn't help but find amusing. All those years of Harvard expectations gone in an instant, replaced by a sense of reprieve so big it seemed to fill every inch of him.

"Besides," he was saying, "he's still too gutted about Harvard to notice anything else. But it's over now. So he'll either get past it or he won't."

"He will," Clare had insisted. "He'll get past it."

But Aidan only shrugged. "Or he won't."

Now Riley is leaning forward, her eyes wide and owlish behind her glasses, which she pushes up on her nose with one finger. "The thing is," she says, her voice just a whisper, "it turns out he never even applied."

Clare stares at her, genuinely shocked. *"What?"*

"I know," Riley says, looking half-horrified by the news and half-thrilled at being the one to deliver it. "Dad's been really upset all summer, but lately he's gotten kind of weirdly obsessive about Harvard again. I think it's because Aidan's about to leave, and he's having a hard time watching him pack up for another school. He's been trying to get over it—he really has—but the other night, he asked to see the rejection letter, I guess just for closure maybe, or I don't know why. But none of us had ever actually seen it...."

"Me neither," Clare admits. They'd only shown each other their acceptances, because the idea of handing over a stack of failures—even just to Aidan—was too much for Clare. She'd stuffed all of hers in the trash within minutes of receiving them, burying all the *so-sorry*s and *thanks-for-trying*s beneath coffee grounds and banana peels, as if somehow that were enough to strike them from the record. There were plenty of others to celebrate. So that's what they did.

"Well, he said he threw it away, but he was being sort of weird about it, so I guess Dad finally decided to call the admissions office today—"

"Why?"

Riley shrugged. "I don't know. Probably to give them a piece of his mind. But it turns out they don't have any record of the application."

"I can't believe he would do that," Clare says, still reeling. But there's something else at the edge of her surprise, something dark and unsettling that she can't quite place until Riley comes right out and says it for her.

"So he really never told you?"

She shakes her head.

"I thought he told you everything."

"Apparently not," Clare says, her voice tight.

"Well, anyway," Riley says, twirling a pen between her fingers, "Dad's really mad at him now. As you can probably imagine."

Clare nods, but her mind is elsewhere. She can't believe Aidan wouldn't have told her. They tell each other everything. Not just the big stuff, but the little things, too: when Clare decided to switch toothpastes, and when Aidan discovered a penny in his shoe; whenever Clare has a dream about clowns, or whenever Aidan remembers to floss. It doesn't matter what it is, whether it's good or bad, hugely important or completely insignificant: The reward for doing pretty much anything, for surviving it or conquering it or just plain getting through it, is getting to tell Aidan about it afterward.

She always thought it was the same for him.

But now she isn't so sure.

Downstairs, they hear a door slam, and then a few muffled

voices. Riley glances up at the clock above her desk, which is shaped like an old-fashioned teapot.

"I told my friends I'd be there by now," she says. "I wonder how much longer this is gonna take."

"Maybe we should try to go rescue him," Clare suggests with more conviction than she feels, and Riley casts a cautious glance at her bedroom door before standing up with a little nod.

They walk downstairs quietly, their footsteps softened by the nubby gray carpet, then tiptoe through the dining room, where the voices from the kitchen become clearer.

"We're just disappointed," Mrs. Gallagher is saying, her tone placating. "You can understand that...."

"You would have been disappointed either way," Aidan says, and there's a hard edge to his voice. "Even if I'd gotten in, it's not like I was ever gonna go. It's what *you* wanted, not me. I was just trying to save us all the trouble of fighting about it."

There's a short pause, and then Mr. Gallagher clears his throat. "That's all fine," he says, though from the tone of his voice, there doesn't seem to be anything fine about it. "But the way you did it, in the sneakiest, most cowardly way possible—"

"It was the *only* way—" Aidan says, but his father interrupts him.

"You think you're so grown up, heading off to college, but you're not—not yet. A real man wouldn't have lied.

A real man wouldn't have taken the easy way out." He pauses, letting out a long sigh. "But you made your decision. There's nothing that can be done about it now. It was your choice, and now you're the one who has to live with it."

Beside Clare, Riley shifts her weight, and a floorboard groans beneath her. Before they can do anything, the door swings open, and they're faced with Mrs. Gallagher, whose lips are pressed into a thin line.

"Sorry," Riley says quickly. "It's just that Aidan promised to drive me—"

"I'm not sure we're quite—" she says, but Mr. Gallagher cuts her off.

"It's fine," he says, and there's something wrenching and final in his voice when he turns to Aidan, who is staring at him with a stubborn expression that Clare knows well, his jaw hard and his eyes blazing. "We're all done here."

But Aidan doesn't move. Nobody does.

"We'll be waiting outside," Riley says after a moment, then she spins around, and Clare follows her back through the dining room and out the front door, where they stumble into the cool evening air, relieved to be out of the house.

Clare takes a seat on the steps, hugging her knees to her chest. It's almost entirely dark now, and the yard is throbbing with the sound of crickets, the neighborhood otherwise quiet all around them. Riley sits down beside her and adopts a similar pose.

"He's an idiot," she says after a minute or so. "But I also sort of get it."

Clare turns to her. "Yeah?"

"It's not that he's a coward. He's just realistic, you know?"

"I know," Clare says, because this is true. Aidan is an optimist at heart, but he's careful about it. He would never spend the time or energy to go after something he had no interest in having. He's much too practical for that, far too economical about his hopes and dreams. If he were going to try for something, it would be for one of two reasons: Either he was certain he could get it or he was certain it was worth it.

"But he's still an idiot," Riley says, giving her a shy smile, " 'cause if he'd gone to Harvard, he could have been closer to you."

Clare closes her eyes. It's been a long time since she's allowed herself this same thought: the two of them shuttling back and forth between Harvard and Dartmouth, a mere two-hour drive, spending weekends skiing in Vermont or picking apples in New Hampshire, going to museums in Boston and watching the boats slip by on the Charles.

She knows this person she's been trying so hard to keep from imagining—the one with the winter coat and clunky snow boots, bundled up and red-cheeked during those cozy New England winters—isn't Aidan. It's not who he is or what he wants. But it still hurts to know that it was never even a possibility, and sitting here in the early darkness of this suburban night, it only makes her feel like it's already here, this looming distance between them, like they've already been set adrift.

"I'm going to miss him," Clare says with a suddenness that startles them both. She gives a helpless shrug, and Riley nods.

"I know," she says. "Me too."

Clare bumps her gently with her shoulder. "And I'll miss you, too."

"Yeah?" Riley asks, her face lighting up.

"Yeah. You'd better keep in touch."

"I will," she says. "I swear. Even if you and Aidan break up."

Clare flinches at the words. This is the whole point of the night, of course, its inevitable end. But still, it sends a little shock through her to hear it said out loud.

Behind them, the door opens, casting a wedge of light over the front stoop, and Aidan steps outside. They both twist to look up at him, and he stands there for a long moment, his eyes distant and blank, rubbing his hands together, though it's not very cold.

Finally, he tips his head down to face them with a smile that's full of effort. "So much for quick and painless," he says with a sheepish expression. "New rule for tonight. No more unscheduled stops."

Clare nods. "Deal."

His face softens when their eyes meet, but his words snap like firecrackers in the dark. "Hi and bye," he says, and she has to swallow the knot in her throat before she can respond.

"Hi and bye."

STOP #5

The Bowling Alley

9:17 PM

As soon as Aidan pulls into one of the many empty parking spots in front of the Incredibowl—where the only truly incredible thing is just how totally outdated the place is—Riley dashes out of the car, tossing off a hasty thank-you before the door slams shut behind her.

"I think she's late to meet her friends," Clare says, watching her trot off through the fog, though she suspects the truth is that Riley's just eager to escape the strained silence in the car, something Clare half wishes she could do as well.

Instead, she remains sitting there beside Aidan, staring out the dirty windshield at the low-slung building, which is wreathed in neon lights, the entrance bookended by two giant bowling pins with chipping paint, standing guard like weary soldiers.

Aidan hasn't said a word since they left his house, and Clare thinks this might be the longest she's ever heard him go quiet. He's not like so many of the other guys in their class, sullen and moody and withdrawn; if there's one thing Aidan Gallagher can do, it's *talk*. He's got a knack for keeping up a steady chatter, and he's never met an awkward silence he couldn't plow through with idle musings. When they're together, it's never mattered whether or not Clare keeps up her end of the conversation. A lot of the time, it doesn't even matter if she's listening. Aidan has a habit of answering his own questions, a sort of absent-minded call-and-response that requires nobody else on the other end.

"Have you ever noticed that girls always seem to fold their socks while guys always roll them?" he'd said just yesterday while watching her pack. "It's interesting, right? I wonder which one is actually more effective. Do you think anyone's ever done a study of that sort of thing? Maybe we should do an experiment right now. Maybe we'll win an award for our work in the field of hyper-efficient packing techniques...."

"Aidan," Clare had said, looking over at him distractedly, "can you *please* shut up?"

"Not a chance," he'd replied good-naturedly; then he'd turned to start emptying the contents of her sock drawer. While she packed up the rest of her things, he dutifully rolled or folded each pair of socks with a look of great concentration, providing color commentary all the while.

That's just Aidan: a natural talker, an unconscious prattler, a cheerful banterer. Though she teases him for it, it's always been comforting, like being armed with a parachute for any kind of potentially uncomfortable social situation. There's simply not room for long pauses when he's around, and Clare—who falls on the quieter end of the spectrum—has always been grateful for that.

But now, after a completely silent fifteen-minute drive to the bowling alley, she's starting to worry that this night—which was supposed to be all about conversation, all about discussion and dialogue and debate—might already be sunk.

In the quiet of the car, she plays with one of her rings, sliding it off her finger and then back on again, waiting for him to do something first: to speak or get out or drive away again. But as the minutes stretch between them with no end in sight, she finally looks over at him.

"Aidan," she says, and he doesn't react. His face is pale in the glow of a nearby streetlamp, and his forehead is creased. "You should've told me...."

When he still doesn't respond, she wonders if he could possibly be thinking they won't talk about what happened, if his plan is just to roll the whole thing up like a pair of socks and tuck it away.

"I would've understood," she says, pressing on, and he leans his head back against the seat, his eyes pinned to the shadowy ceiling of the car.

"Like you do now?" he asks in a flat tone that doesn't even sound like him.

They're not accustomed to fighting, and when they've done so, it's always had a slightly playful edge to it, more sparring than actual combat. They'd once made a pact to differentiate between Petty High School Dramas and Big Life Issues, swearing that they'd only ever argue when it was something important, something that really mattered. But now that they're here, now that the stage is bigger and the discussion has widened and they can't seem to find their way through, Clare wonders if maybe they're not equipped for the Big Life Issues after all. Maybe they never were.

"That's not fair," she says in a voice that sounds way too reasonable. "We haven't even talked about it yet."

"Yeah, but I know you, Clare Rafferty," he says, still without looking at her. "I know you like things a certain way. You would've loved to be the girl at Dartmouth with the Harvard boyfriend."

"That's not—"

He shakes his head. "I know you've been great about UCLA. You have. But if Harvard had been an option—a real on-the-table option—I honestly don't know whether you would've been on my side."

Clare stares at him, stung by this. "Of *course* I would have," she says, even as a part of her wonders if that's true. The fact that he didn't even try to get in—not to mention that he didn't tell her—feels like a kind of rejection.

But what if he *had* been accepted? If there was a chance for them to be closer next year—if he could have chosen Harvard, chosen the East Coast, chosen *her*, but *didn't*— isn't it possible she would've felt differently?

Last fall, when Aidan was constantly complaining about Harvard, Clare had made him a deal. "If you stop moaning and groaning about being forced to apply to the best academic institution in the country," she said, "I'll put in an application for somewhere I don't want to go, either."

It had turned into a game, the two of them poring over heavy books filled with rankings and seemingly endless online lists. Aidan's first suggestions were all jokes, places that were much too close (the community college that Scotty's now attending), or much too far (universities in Moscow and Tokyo and Beijing), much too technical (MIT), or not technical enough (a college of "living wisdom" where you could actually major in yoga).

But once Clare had nixed all of those, Aidan got serious.

"All your others are on the East Coast," he pointed out. "So maybe we should find you something out west to balance things out."

"I like that," she'd said. "That way, we'll sort of be mirroring each other, since you're all West Coast except for Harvard."

After that, it was easy. Finding the closest thing to Harvard on the West Coast meant one thing: Stanford. And so she'd applied.

When her rejection arrived, Clare didn't mind. She'd never expected to get in, nor had she ever seriously considered going there, but she was surprised to see a flicker of disappointment in Aidan's eyes when she told him.

"Well, there goes our safety school."

Clare had frowned. "Stanford wasn't my safety. Not by a long shot."

"Yeah," he said, smiling, "but it was mine."

"You applied?" she asked, staring at him, and he shook his head.

"There was just something kind of cool about knowing we might be on the same coast," he told her. "Kind of like a safety net...you know, for us."

"Well, there's always Harvard," she said, expecting that to cheer him up a bit, but instead, she saw something shut down behind his eyes, and he only shrugged.

"We'll see."

Clare doesn't mind that he didn't end up applying. Not really. She knows that Aidan's best and worst quality is this: that he wants everyone to be happy. He's always bending over backward, doing cartwheels and flips and somersaults in an effort to make sure he doesn't offend anyone. So she can understand his logic. If he'd applied and gotten into Harvard, there's no way he could have chosen another school without causing a huge rift with his father. But if he fixed the odds himself, making sure it wasn't even a possibility, there was a chance he could get out of the trap that had been set for him his entire life with barely a scratch.

Only it hadn't worked.

And worse, he'd left her completely in the dark.

That's what she minds: that he hadn't told her, that he hadn't trusted her enough to believe she'd be supportive. After nearly two years together—two whole years of being the most important person in each other's lives—this feels like a kick in the teeth.

"Aidan," she says now, her eyes trained on his shadowy profile in the dim light of the car. "I'm *always* on your side. But you can't put me in the same category as your parents. You can't lie to me just because you're afraid of how I might react."

"I didn't lie."

She fixes him with a hard look. "You're doing it again right now."

"I didn't..." he begins, then stops and blows out a long breath. "I didn't *mean* to lie. At least not to you."

"Then why did you?" she asks, feeling her throat tighten a little. "I would've understood."

"Maybe," he says grudgingly. "It's easy to say that now."

"Still."

He shrugs. "I guess I felt bad about the Stanford thing."

"Yeah, but that was never serious," Clare tells him, sitting forward. "And I knew Harvard wasn't, either."

"Did you?"

"Yes," she says firmly, then hesitates, because she knows the only way to get through this is for her to be honest, too. "I mean, maybe there was this tiny little part of me that—"

He doesn't even wait for her to finish. "See?"

"But that's not the point," she says, trying to curb her frustration. "If you'd told me you were scrapping the application, I would've understood. I would've been supportive either way."

"Yeah, but—"

"Aidan," she says, cutting him off, "you should've just been honest with me."

He traces a finger along the ridges of the steering wheel, then leans forward and rests his head against it. "Why are we still talking about this? It doesn't even matter anymore. It would've turned out the same either way."

"Yeah, but we're supposed to be a team. After all this time, you should've had more faith in me."

"Right. Like you have in *us*?"

Clare opens her mouth, then closes it again, not sure what to say to that. Instead, she falls back against the seat with a sigh, and they're both silent for a minute, then two.

"The thing is," Aidan says eventually, "maybe I don't."

"Don't what?"

"Have enough faith in you."

This hits her like a shot—a hard, bright pain in the center of her chest—and she struggles to keep her face neutral. "Then maybe," she says, unable to look at him, "we have bigger problems."

"Maybe we do," he says, moving a hand to the door. He glances over at her, and there's a flicker of impatience in his eyes. "Are we done yet?"

"What?"

"I don't feel like talking about this anymore."

"Aidan," she says. "Come on. You can't just keep avoiding everything."

"And you can't just keep planning everything," he says,

sounding uncharacteristically surly. "This isn't a home-work assignment. There's not gonna be an answer for everything, okay? There's just not."

He opens his car door, and when the overhead light snaps on, they both blink like stunned animals.

Clare glances at the green numbers of the dashboard clock. "So, what?" she says in a low voice. "Your plan is just to spend the rest of the night pretending nothing hap-pened? You just want to—what? Go bowling right now?"

"You're the one who brought me here," he says, stepping out of the car. She shoves open her own door, then hops out and glares at him from across the hood.

"We can leave if you want."

Without answering, he begins to cross the parking lot, punching the lock button from over his shoulder. Clare flinches as the car lets out two shrill beeps, then hurries after him toward the giant bowling pins at the entrance.

"So what is it, anyway?" Aidan asks, pausing just as they reach the door. Inside, the orange light of the lanes gives off a faint glow, and they can hear the cheerful music of the video games in the lobby.

"What do you mean?"

"On the list," he says. "What is this on the list?"

She frowns at him. "You don't remember?"

He remains silent, but there's something deliberately stubborn about it.

"Yes, you do," she tells him, digging in, too.

"Not really," he says, just as a group of middle-aged

men in blue bowling shirts, their names stitched above the pockets, come lumbering out the door, causing Aidan and Clare to take a step back and away from each other.

When they're gone, he turns back to her with glassy eyes.

"So?" he asks, and she shakes her head, exhausted.

"Forget it," she says, pulling open the door and walking inside without him, happy to let the noise and lights of the place wash over her: the bright sound of the balls striking the pins, the clinking of glasses, and the confusion of voices, all of it a hazy, welcome distraction.

Aidan stalks off toward the snack bar, but Clare stops near the shoe-rental booth, scanning the lanes to see if she recognizes anyone other than Riley, who is wedged on a bench with a couple of her friends, bent forward as she laces up her shoes.

"Hey," says a familiar voice behind her, and Clare turns to find Stella balancing two plastic cups and a bag of popcorn under one arm. "I didn't realize you guys were coming here."

"Riley needed a lift," Clare says, rescuing the popcorn, which is spilling onto the ugly patterned carpet one kernel at a time.

Stella scans the room. "Where's Aidan?"

"No clue," Clare says shortly.

"O-kay. Well, we're over there with Mike and Noah and Kip. They've been here for ages, and they're completely—" She's using one of the cups to point in the direction of the far lanes, but when she notices Aidan is already over there, she lowers her hand and turns back to Clare with a sheepish look. "Guess we found Aidan."

"Guess so," Clare says, aware of the edge to her voice.

"Everything okay? You seem a little..."

"Annoyed?"

"I was gonna say pissed, but sure, annoyed."

"Aidan's..." She hesitates, not sure how to finish that sentence. "An idiot."

"Is that all?" Stella asks, laughing. "He's always been an idiot. You can't break up with him because of *that*. It's a preexisting condition."

"We haven't broken up," Clare says quickly, surprised at the way her heart picks up speed at the thought. "We're still just..."

"Talking," Stella says.

"Talking," she agrees.

"Were you at your house?"

"His," she says. "And we stopped by the beach, too."

"Don't suppose you managed to save poor Rusty?"

Clare manages a small smile. "No. I think he's just gonna have to survive on his own till we all get back at Thanksgiving."

"So is Scotty," Stella says, her expression turning serious. "And I'm not sure he's handling it so well."

"He'll be fine. He's Scotty. He's always fine."

"I guess," Stella says, though she doesn't sound quite convinced. Her eyes drift back to where the boys are all gathered around the scoring machine at the very last lane, and Clare watches her carefully.

"Why are you so worried about *Scotty*?" she says, and Stella looks back at her, surprised.

"I don't know," she says. "I'm not."

"You hate Scotty," Clare reminds her. "You guys aren't even really friends."

"Yeah, but—"

"You and me," she says, feeling suddenly annoyed, "we've been friends our whole lives."

"I know."

"And we're both leaving tomorrow."

Stella looks unsure about where this might be headed. "Yeah..."

"So why don't you try caring about *that* for a minute?" Clare asks with a frown, and in the quiet that follows, they stare at each other, both a little stunned by the words, which sounded harsher than intended. But it's a thought that's been stuck in the back of Clare's throat for a while now; it was only a matter of time before it came tumbling out.

"I do," Stella says in an appeasing tone.

"Not really. You haven't been around for weeks. And until tonight, you've barely even bothered to ask about the whole Aidan thing."

"That's because we've been talking about it for *months*."

"Yeah, but that was all just hypothetical. Now it's actually happening. Now is when I actually need you."

Stella lifts her shoulders. "I'm right here."

"No, you're not," Clare says, shaking her head. "Not really. And it's too late, anyway."

"Hey, I'm sorry if—"

"Forget it," Clare says, cutting her off. She blinks at her friend, feeling a lump rise in her throat. Because this isn't the way their last night was supposed to go. She and Stella have been inseparable since they were little. They'd sat together in kindergarten, learned to ride bikes the same day, thrown joint birthday parties as kids. They'd shared books and lunches, stickers and clothes—at least until eighth grade, when Stella had decided that black was her color. They'd shared pretty much everything.

All this time, they'd been running a marathon together. And now, with only yards left to go, Stella has fallen away, and Clare can't for the life of her figure out why.

"You haven't been there," she says, trying to keep her lip from trembling. "You were supposed to be there."

"Clare."

"No, it's fine," she says, giving Stella a hard look. "This is just part of it, right? I guess we're supposed to be moving on."

"Not like this."

Clare shrugs, and a few pieces of popcorn fall to the floor. "Starting next week, none of this will matter, anyway. We'll each have a whole new group of friends...."

"What, like Beatrice St. James?" Stella asks, arching an eyebrow.

"Well, yeah," Clare says. "Maybe. Probably."

"Clare, come on."

"No, maybe it's better this way. Maybe we just have to learn to stop needing each other so much."

She waits for Stella to disagree, or to tell her she's being stupid, but she doesn't. Instead, her shoulders slump, and she stares down at the drinks in her hands for what feels like a very long time. Then, finally, she looks right at Clare.

"Maybe you're right," she says, entirely blank-faced, and then, without another word, she brushes past her, hurrying down the steps to the lanes.

Clare stands there, watching her go, her feet strangely heavy. After a moment, she takes a shaky breath.

Fine, she thinks. *One less goodbye.*

It's supposed to make her lighter, this thought, but all she feels is hollow as she starts to walk in the direction of her friends, picking her way around the discarded shoes that litter the sticky floor.

As she approaches the last lane, she can see that the rest of the guys—Noah and Mike and Kip—are messing around with the scoreboard, picking ridiculous names for everyone, and Scotty is staggering around with a hot-pink bowling ball under his arm, doubled over in laughter.

Only Aidan is standing apart, still scowling at nothing in particular, and when Clare tries to catch his eye, he just folds his arms across his chest and looks off toward the six pins still upright at the end of the lane.

"Hey, Stells," Scotty says, swaying slightly in the way

that he does when he's drunk. Clare raises her eyebrows at the nickname, but Stella only rolls her eyes at him as he attempts to spin the bowling ball on his finger like a basketball. It falls to the floor with a bone-rattling *thud*. "I've got a joke for you."

"What is it?" Clare asks when nobody else does. With both Aidan and Stella acting like jerks, she feels a sudden surge of affection for Scotty. He looks so eager, standing there in his red-and-blue bowling shoes, which he bought last year, even though he's a truly terrible bowler. He ended up loving them so much that he started wearing them to school, sliding up and down the hallways between classes.

"Why is a bowling alley the quietest place on earth?" he asks, looking pleased with himself. He doesn't have the patience to wait for an answer. He just rushes on, eager to tell them. "Because you can hear a pin drop!"

Clare can't help laughing a little at this, but Stella just shakes her head, walking over to scoop up the bowling ball. Aidan ignores him entirely, glancing up to check the score on the screens overhead, where his name is now listed as A-Dog and Clare's is C-Money. Nobody else seems to notice except for Scotty, who takes a few lurching steps in Aidan's direction, scowling at him.

"What?" he says, his face a little too red. "Not funny enough for you?"

Aidan turns around, clearly surprised. "Just not in the mood for jokes, I guess."

"Why not?" Scotty demands. "Did you guys finally break up or something?"

"Scotty," Stella says, taking him by the arm before he can reach for his cup again. She shoves the pink bowling ball at him, and he lets out a little grunt as it hits him in the stomach. "I think you're up."

"No, Kip's not done," he says, pointing at the six pins still standing, but Kip—who has been watching this all unfold with benign amusement—waves an arm.

"All you, big guy," he says with a lazy smile. "You can finish up for me."

Scotty shrugs, then saunters up to the lane, turning once to wink at them before tossing the ball straight into the gutter. He stands there watching it whizz away, steady as a pinball, and once it disappears at the end of the lane, he turns around with his arms raised in triumph.

Out of the corner of her eye, Clare notices Riley waving at her from somewhere in the middle of all the lanes, and she lifts a hand to wave back. But when she hears a roar of laughter behind her, she realizes Scotty has seen her, too.

"Is that why you're in such a terrible mood, buddy?" he asks Aidan with an off-kilter grin, once again in good humor. "Because your sister followed me here?"

"Cut it out, Scotty," Aidan says, giving him a hard look. Clare can see that his face is flushed behind his freckles, and she knows that this is the quickest way to rankle him, not because it's a real possibility anymore—Scotty and Riley—but because he's protective and a little bit sensitive and, most of all, because he's a good older brother, all things she usually admires about him.

But tonight isn't the night to tease him about it, and she widens her eyes and shakes her head at Scotty, trying to communicate this to him, though she knows it's probably hopeless. He's still smiling, a goofy, lopsided smile, and she can tell he's only just warming up.

"What can I do?" he says, all innocence and charm, his hair sticking up at the back in a way that makes him look like a cartoon character. "You know how the girls all love me. It's not her fault she can't stay away...."

"Grow up," Aidan says, spinning around to leave. He takes two long strides, then stops and turns back again, and Clare can tell that he's gone from annoyed to angry, something that usually only happens when he's arguing with his father. "Actually, forget it. You're never gonna grow up, are you? There's a reason you're getting left behind in this stupid town with all these stupid high schoolers. It's because you still act like one."

He pauses for a second, licking his lips, and then glances at Clare, a little wild-eyed, before turning back to Scotty.

"You know what?" Aidan says to him in a low voice. "You belong here."

For a moment it feels like everything stops, though around them people continue to go about their games, bowling and cheering and drinking and laughing as if Aidan hadn't just said the exact wrong thing, as if he hadn't just bulldozed his way right through to his best friend's worst fears: that not only do they all feel sorry for him, but that nobody is surprised he's the one to be left behind.

All the color has drained from Scotty's face, and Clare stares at Aidan, who looks a bit stricken himself. She's seized by the memory of the first time they came here together, a few months after they started dating, when—after a night of gutter balls and one-pin shots and endless jokes at her expense about the merits of bumper bowling—she'd somehow managed to throw a wobbly and slow-moving strike.

The minute the pins fell, she turned and ran back to the benches with her hands in the air, and before she could say anything, before she could even catch her breath, Aidan had wrapped her in a bear hug, lifting her off her feet and twirling her around, both of them laughing.

When he set her down again, his eyes were shining, and he leaned in close. "I *love* you," he'd said, like a kid declaring his feelings for ice cream or bugs or the circus, full of wonder and delight.

Now she realizes she's standing in the exact same spot, and once again, Aidan is looking at her, only this time his face is completely blank, and something about the emptiness of his gaze makes Clare go cold.

Stella is the first to react. "God, Aidan," she says, moving closer to Scotty. "You don't have to be such a prick about it."

"It's fine," Scotty says gruffly, but his eyes are on the floor.

Clare is about to say something to Aidan—though she doesn't know what yet—when he turns abruptly and starts walking away. She stares after him, shocked that he would leave this unfinished, and on this of all nights. They've gotten into countless scuffles before, Aidan and Scotty, but it's always ended in laughter. Always. Now, though, something feels different. Everything is too fraught, too weighty, too final.

"I'm sorry," Clare says, whirling back around. "He's just—he's not in great form right now. But he shouldn't be taking it out on everyone else."

"It's fine," Scotty says again.

Clare looks back toward the exit, half expecting to find that Aidan is gone, but instead, she sees that he's pacing in front of the doors, his head bent and his shoulders curled. She starts to head over to him but then stops, frozen with indecision.

"Go," Stella says, and though her eyes are still hard, her voice is gentle. "He's an idiot. But he's your idiot."

Clare stares at her for a moment, then nods. "Maybe we'll see you guys later," she says without much conviction, and Stella simply lifts a hand in a kind of half wave. It's impossible to tell whether it means goodbye for now or goodbye for good, and Clare doesn't stay to find out. Instead, she sets the bag of popcorn on the table, then turns and jogs over toward the exit, her blood pumping loud in her ears.

When she reaches Aidan, he greets her not with an apology or an explanation but just a stubbornly, maddeningly distant expression, and she walks right up to him and jabs a finger into the soft cotton of his shirt, right in the middle of his chest.

"It's where you first said you loved me," she says a little breathlessly, hoping to jolt him out of this, to remind him, to reel him back. "That's why we're here."

But when she looks up at him, his eyes are so sad that it pulls her up short. In the silence that follows, it's almost as if Scotty's stupid joke has come true. Behind them, pins are crashing to the ground over and over again with a sound like thunder, like something shattering, but right here, in the muffled space between them, it might as well be the quietest place on earth.

"Yeah, well," Aidan says eventually, just before walking out the door into a dusting of rain, "it's not like you've ever said it back."

STOP #6

The Mini-Mart

9:41 PM

When she doesn't find him by the car, Clare walks back around to the side of the building, where Aidan is sitting on the curb, his head bent over his phone. There's a faint rotten smell coming from the nearby trash bins, blown in their direction by the rain: a fine, clinging mist that feels good after the closeness of the bowling alley.

Clare stands over him for a few seconds, but when he doesn't show any sign of acknowledging her, she finally joins him on the curb, leaving a few inches between them.

"I'm sorry," she says, tilting her head to look at him. "I didn't know it still bothered you."

Aidan laughs, but there's nothing funny in the sound of it. "That you don't love me?"

"That I don't say it."

"Same thing."

"It's not," she insists, as she's done so many times before. "You know how I feel about you."

"See," he says, "that's the problem. Maybe I don't."

"Aidan."

"No wonder you think we should break up," he says, his eyes flashing with anger. "If you can't say it now, you probably never will."

"I've told you," she says, grinding the heels of her hands against her eyes, already feeling defeated by an argument she's never going to win. "I don't want to say it unless it's—"

"True?" he asks. "Real?"

She shakes her head, frustrated. "Unless it's forever."

"Right," he says, looking hurt. "And this isn't. Message received."

They're both silent after that, and Clare closes her eyes. She'd give just about anything not to be talking about this. Not tonight. Not when they only have so many hours left. Especially since she knows the only thing she can say to make it better is the one thing she still can't bring herself to voice.

For a long time, Aidan hadn't seemed to mind. Shortly after he'd first said it—right here at the bowling alley— they'd spent an afternoon at an art museum downtown. There was a special Picasso exhibition, and Clare had stopped to study a painting of a child holding a white dove.

"Looks like true dove to me," Aidan had joked, coming up behind her.

"Definitely dove at first sight."

"You know what I dove? Paintings of doves."

She smiled. "Oh, yeah?"

"And actual doves," he said as she turned, slipping her arms around his neck. "Who doesn't dove doves, right?"

"I dove *you*," she'd said, rising onto her tiptoes to kiss him. And for a while, that had been enough.

I dove you, Clare had said a week later, the words bubbling up inside her as she watched him scramble around on the floor of the grocery store after his bag of apples had split open. *I dove you*, she'd shouted above the noise, after he'd kissed her in the wild, celebratory aftermath of a lacrosse win, and she'd said it again during the quiet moment just before they parted on an ordinary Tuesday night in her driveway.

I dove you, I dove you, I dove you.

It was just one letter off, but to Clare, it came from the same place. Swapping out a *D* for an *L* shouldn't have mattered—not when all the right feelings were there—but for some reason, it did. It felt safer, somehow, less permanent. Because love wasn't something you could take back. It was like a magic spell: Once you said the words, they were simply out there, shifting and changing everything that had once been true.

All her life, Clare has watched her parents pass the word back and forth as if it weren't a fragile object, as if it were the sturdiest thing in the world. They've never been content to say it just once. "I love love love you," her dad calls to her mom each morning as he walks out the door, and she always yells it back to him the same way: "I love love love you."

Clare had asked them about it once, when she was little, and they'd just smiled and said it was because they loved each other three times as much as anyone else.

But later, when she was old enough for the story—nine years old and starting to ask questions—they sat her down to explain the truth about their history, about how they'd each been married once before.

"But why?" Clare had asked at the time, trying to absorb the idea that not only had her parents had lives before her, but that they'd also had lives before *each other*. It was mind-boggling to try to imagine a time when they hadn't been a family, when there weren't pancakes on the table every Sunday morning, when their names weren't written in the sidewalk out front, when their shoes weren't strewn beside the back door.

"Why..." she'd asked, blinking back tears, feeling like the whole world had gone sideways. "Why didn't you just *wait* for each other?"

"We were young," her mom had explained gently, stroking Clare's hair. "We thought we'd both found real love. But really, it was just first love."

"Things change when you get older," her dad said. "But we were lucky. For us, second love turned out to be the best kind." He reached out and took her mom's hand. "Which is why I don't just love your mom. I love love *love* her."

"Why three, then?" Clare asked. "If it's only the second?"

"Because two isn't nearly enough," her dad said with a smile. "But if I said it a thousand times, I'd be late to work."

Clare is aware that her parents aren't normal—not because they're both divorced, but because they're so bizarrely happy now. What she doesn't know is whether that's because they're just lucky—because they've been fortunate enough to find each other in spite of making a mistake the first time around—or whether what they say is true: that second love is the best kind.

But either way, something about this has made her overly cautious when it comes to love. There's too much uncertainty, too many chances to make mistakes.

And she doesn't ever want Aidan to be a mistake.

So no matter how strong her feelings for him, she refuses to rush the words. They're too significant, too definite, too lasting. When she finally says them, she wants it to be to the first, last, and only person. She wants it to count.

"Yeah, but you actually say it all the time," Aidan once pointed out as they stood at the sink, washing some vegetables they'd brought home from the farmers' market in town. "You say it to your parents. And to Bingo."

Clare had rolled her eyes. "That's different. He's a dog."

"So, what, I just need to beg more?" he'd joked, starting to get down on his knees, right there on her kitchen floor. She'd caught him by the elbow and pulled him up again, kissing him instead.

"No begging," she'd said, in the same firm tone she always used to scold the dog.

But now it's been like this for so long—a careful joke, a fragile understanding—that she's completely caught off guard by his reaction tonight.

She swivels to face him more fully, but he still refuses to meet her eye. "I might not say it, but I obviously show you how I feel," she says. "Why do the words have to be so important?"

"They just are," he says, standing up and brushing off the back of his jeans. "Not because you're saying them, but because you're *not*."

When he starts to walk away, she stands up, too. "I don't get why you're so upset about this *now*," she says, jogging after him. "I didn't think you cared before—"

He stops abruptly. "God, Clare. Of course I cared. How many times do you think someone can say *I love you* without hearing it back?"

Her heart falls at this, because all his anger is stripped away now, and what's left is just pure hurt.

"I'm sorry," she says, reaching for his hand, but he pulls it back, then turns to the car, fumbling for his keys.

"I used to think it was just another one of your stupid rules," he says with his back to her. The shoulders of his shirt are damp from the rain, and his hair glistens with it. "But now I'm not so sure."

Clare blinks at him, feeling leaden straight down to her toes. However prepared she thought she'd been to break up with him tonight, she realizes now that she hadn't *really* expected it to happen. At least not like this. Not in the way that most couples break up: fighting and scrabbling, dredging up long-dormant arguments and lobbing them at each other like grenades. If it had to end, she'd imagined it would be poignant and inevitable: a single tear, a sorrowful hug, a brave goodbye.

But Aidan is already in the car, the engine humming to life, and there's nothing for her to do but hurry around to the other side and get in, too, worried that he might actually leave without her. When she does, he lurches out of the spot without a word, his hands tight on the wheel, his mouth set in a straight line.

It isn't until they're nearly back to the main part of town that he clears his throat, a rattling noise that makes Clare jump a little.

"Where to?" he asks, and she lifts a shoulder.

"Wherever you want."

"What about the list?"

She glances over at him. "It feels kind of silly now," she says quietly, and he doesn't disagree.

When the light changes, he takes a left. "I need to get gas."

"Okay," she says with a bit too much enthusiasm. It's just a relief to have a next step. She takes a deep breath, then tries again. "That sounds good."

The gas station is on the edge of town, a small patch of uneven asphalt with six rusted pumps. Behind them, there's a darkened car wash and a mini-mart where, through the window, they can see a bored-looking attendant flipping through a magazine at the counter.

Aidan hops out without a word, crossing in front of the car to reach the fuel tank, which is on Clare's side. While he adjusts the hose, she pulls out her phone, giving the inside of the car a faint glow. It's just after ten o'clock, and what had before seemed like it would be the shortest night of her life—marked by too many things to say and too many places to go—now looms ahead of her, endless and full of uncertainty.

As he waits for the tank to fill up, Aidan leans against her window, the back of his blue plaid shirt pressed flat against the glass. Normally, she'd do something like roll the window down to startle him, and then he'd do something like whip around and surprise her by wielding a squeegee, threatening to drip it on her until she got out to help him, and then they'd spend the time until the pump clicked soaping up the windows of his perpetually dirty car.

But not tonight.

Tonight, she just sits there, quietly waiting.

She's deep enough inside her own head that when someone knocks on the driver's-side window, she makes a startled noise. When she looks over to find a police officer peering in, her stomach lurches and, reflexively, her face goes hot with a guilty flush.

But the man is smiling at her expectantly, and after a beat, Clare realizes that she actually knows him: It's her friend Allie's dad. It's been a while since she's seen him, and she's surprised that he even recognized her. The last thing she feels like right now is small talk, but she leans across the car to roll down the window anyway.

"Hi, Officer Lerner," she says with a little wave. She and Allie were best friends in elementary school, and though they've since grown apart, pulled into different social circles somewhere around the start of junior high, they've always remained friendly in the way you do with anyone who's witnessed such a significant slice of your past.

"Hey, Clare," he says, leaning his forearms on the window. "Getting ready to head off soon?"

"Tomorrow morning, actually."

"How're your parents taking it?"

"Oh, I think they'll survive," she tells him, but he runs a hand over the back of his beefy neck with a rueful look.

"I wouldn't be too sure about that," he says. "Allie left last week, and I'll tell you what: Her mother and I are at loose ends. It feels like I'm missing my right arm."

"I'm sure she's missing you, too," Clare assures him as Aidan finishes up at the pump and walks back around the front of the car.

"Hi there, young man," Officer Lerner says. "You showing Clare a nice time on her last night?"

"Yes, sir," Aidan says, sticking out his hand. "It's mine, too, actually."

"Last night," he says, nodding appreciatively. "That's big, huh?"

From where she's sitting in the car, Clare can only see Aidan through the bug-speckled windshield, and she watches as he bobs his head a few times.

"You know," Officer Lerner says, "I met Allie's mother when I was in high school."

"Oh, yeah?" Aidan says, cutting his eyes in Clare's direction.

She knows what he's thinking.

He's thinking: *See?*

He's thinking: *I told you so.*

He's thinking: *It can happen.*

But Clare only looks away.

It's true that the world is full of signs. They just mean different things to different people.

To Clare, this looks like the exception.

To Aidan, it looks like the rule.

"Love of my life," Officer Lerner says with a wink, then taps the hood of the car once and steps back. "Though I'd better get going. If anyone spots me hanging around here too long, she'll think I've been buying candy again, and she'll have my neck for that." He pats his chest pocket, which rustles, then winks at them again. "You two enjoy your last night, okay? Stay out of trouble."

"We will," Clare promises.

When he's gone, Aidan slips back into the driver's seat and then sits there for what seems like a very long time without turning the key. As she waits, the silence starts to feel like something tangible, so thick it's hard to breathe, and her face has gone warm in the too-small car. She moves to roll down her window, then changes her mind.

"Gum," she says, her mouth a little chalky. "I need gum."

Aidan frowns. "Okay."

"Be right back," she says, pushing open the door and gulping in the cool air as she weaves between the pumps.

Ahead of her, the mini-mart is like a brightly lit fishbowl in the surrounding darkness, and inside, it smells like an odd mix of gasoline and hot dogs. As she wanders up and down the aisles of chips and candy, the packaging electric-looking under the too-harsh lights, her heart beats fast at the thought of returning to the car.

They'd had a fight here once. It wasn't their first, and it wasn't their biggest, but it had trailed them all the way from Aidan's house, where his father had—as usual—been on his case about his grades, which were always hovering somewhere between decent and pretty good, not because he wasn't smart, but because he didn't care enough to try. As they drove away, Clare couldn't quite bring herself to disagree with Mr. Gallagher.

"If you spent even half the energy you do on the lacrosse field..." she'd said, and Aidan shot her a look.

"It's just as important," he said. "We both know I'm not getting into college because of my grades."

"Not if you don't try," she agreed as they pulled up to the gas station.

It had only escalated from there, and by the time they walked into the mini-mart, they were barely speaking.

But after a few minutes wandering separate aisles, both of them still stewing, Clare felt something hit her lightly between her shoulder blades, and she spun around to find a box of Nerds on the floor at her feet.

When she looked up again, Aidan was smiling at her from the other side of a display of chips. "You're right," he said, then pointed at the box. "I'll try harder. I promise to be more of a nerd."

Clare glanced at the rack of candy bars closest to her and tossed him a roll of Smarties. "You're already a nerd," she told him. "And you're already smart. You just need to put in the time."

"I know," he admitted.

She held up a Payday with a grin. "A reward for hitting the books."

He threw a 100 Grand in her direction. "What's it worth to you?"

"Go fish," she said, winging a package of Swedish Fish at him, and by the time the cashier had kicked them out of the store, they were both laughing so hard they didn't care.

Now the door opens behind her with a mechanical chime, and Clare turns to see Aidan standing there, looking a little dazed. He opens his mouth to say something, then snaps it shut again, and Clare is gripped by a sudden regret at the way the night has unfolded. It feels as if they're on the brink of something they might not be able to take back, and she takes a quick step toward him, still not

106

sure what she's going to say. Behind her, the man at the register drums his fingers hard on the counter.

"You gonna buy that?" he asks, and Clare looks down, realizing that she's holding a pack of gum in her clenched fist. When she uncurls her fingers to look at it, she feels like laughing. She tosses it to Aidan, who snags it easily, then holds it up to read the label. Once he does, his whole body seems to relax, and he raises his eyebrows.

"Ice Breakers?" he says, and she shrugs.

He takes a few steps in her direction, and for a moment, in spite of everything, she wonders if he might kiss her, right here in the mini-mart. But instead, he stops in front of the candy display, scanning the rows of neatly stacked boxes and bags until he finds what he's looking for, and when he hands it to Clare, she realizes it's even better.

Not just one kiss, but a whole package.

STOP #7

The Fountain

10:21 PM

They walk to a soundtrack of crinkling plastic and fluttering wrappers, swapping colors and flavors, exchanging chocolate for gummy bears and licorice for gum. There's more back in the car, which they left tucked in a parking spot behind the mini-mart, but they couldn't carry it all. It had been an impulsive, giddy buying spree, the two of them laughing as they tossed candy onto the counter, the packages skidding like hockey pucks toward the surprised cashier.

Some of the names could have a larger meaning, if you looked at them just right—the wax lips and the candy hearts, even the Chuckles—but most of them didn't. It was just that they'd gotten a little carried away, relieved to be doing something—anything—together, to be reveling in laughter rather than sulking in silence, a happy reprieve, if not a permanent one.

"I have no idea why I'm eating so many of these," Clare says, popping another M&M into her mouth as they cross the street. "I'm not even hungry."

"Me neither," Aidan says cheerfully. "We're definitely gonna get sick."

They haven't discussed a destination, but once they hit the first few shops on the edge of town—the bakery and the jewelry store and the bank that gives out free popcorn on Saturdays—their options are few enough that they both know where they're headed all the same. They pass a couple about their parents' age leaving an Italian restaurant, and they can see down the street to where the lights are still blazing in the windows of Slices, but for the most part, the town is empty at this hour, quiet and still and pretty much all theirs.

At the village square—a rectangular green surrounded by rows of shops on three sides—they head straight for the stone fountain at the center, where the shallow water is littered with pennies, glinting like stars in the moonlight. The rain has stopped now, but there's still the memory of it in the air, which smells as damp and cool as spring. They hoist themselves onto the ledge, their legs dangling as the water burbles at their backs.

"Remember the first time we came here?" Aidan asks, shaking the bag of Skittles in his hand. His eyes are on the train station across the street, where a few people are milling around on the platform, waiting for a late ride into the city.

This time, it's Clare's turn to be confused. "Not really," she says, trying to think back. They've sometimes wandered over as a group after grabbing a bite at Slices, but she can't remember a specific moment with Aidan, nothing meaningful enough that it would have earned a spot on the list.

"We weren't together yet," Aidan says, passing her a few Skittles. "But I liked you. A lot. And Scotty had the idea to get ice cream, but he didn't have any money—"

"Oh, yeah," Clare says, giving him a light whack on the shoulder as it comes back to her. "So he waded in to collect a bunch of change."

"And you started splashing him, which turned into a big water fight."

"I totally remember that. I just forgot you were there."

"I find that impossible to believe," he says with a grin. "I'm completely and totally unforgettable. Not to mention the fact that—"

"Aidan," she says, and he pauses right on the cusp of a speech.

"Yeah?"

"Shut up."

He laughs. "Fine," he says. "But you always think you were the one to notice me first. Clearly I noticed you, too, though. Before we were anything."

Clare lifts her eyes to the moon, which is bluish and nearly full, big as a spotlight and almost as bright. "Before we were anything," she repeats, leaning back to trail her fingers through the cool water. "It seems like a long time ago."

Aidan nods, scratching at his chin. "Hey," he says. "I'm sorry about earlier."

"It's okay."

"Not really," he says. "It's just that my dad made me—"

"You don't have to explain. It's *my* fault. I don't know why I'm so weird about saying it. They're just three stupid little words, right?"

"Well," he says with a smile, "they're not the stupidest."

"I don't know," Clare says. "I mean...*I* is kind of silly, right? Bringing only one letter to the table seems like a pretty weak move."

"And how about *you*?" he says, laughing. "Three letters when one of them already says it all?"

But they end it there. Neither is ready to say anything about the final word, the one sandwiched between the other two, though it hovers there anyway, as hard to ignore as if it were written across the sky in blinking red lights.

Clare swirls her hand through the water once more, then pats it dry on her dress. "I just realized I forgot to get a souvenir at the bowling alley."

"It wasn't exactly our finest moment," Aidan says, turning to look at her. "I'm not sure it's something you'll want to remember."

"I want to remember it all," she says.

In the distance, the sound of a train whistle cuts through the night, and a half second later the bells on the signal lights begin to chime. When the train arrives with a rush of noise, coming to a clattering halt, they watch as a few people step off, then cross through the shadows of the streetlights to their cars.

"Do you ever imagine living here?" Aidan asks, tracking the train as it pulls away again, the red lights growing more distant. "Not like we do now. But the way our parents do. Coming home on the train after work, making dinner, having a house and a yard and all that stuff. Gardening on the weekends."

"Gardening?"

"Well, raking leaves, maybe."

She shakes her head. "You know that's not—"

"I know," he says, holding up his hands. "You're gonna be off doing something brilliant. You'll be some kind of lawyer or banker or journalist, with this crazy apartment in a big city. You're gonna take over the world. But after that..."

"After I take over the world?" she says with a smile. "I might be kind of tired after that."

"You know what I mean."

She lifts her shoulders. "You don't want that, either. Not really."

"You're the one with all the potential. What else do I have to do?"

"Besides gardening?"

He rolls his eyes. "Seriously. I love playing lacrosse. And I'm psyched that I get to do it for four more years. But let's be honest. It's not a career."

"You never know. You said there's a sports-management program at UCLA, right? That sounds up your alley."

"Yeah, but it's just a summer thing, not a real major," he says. "Besides, who knows if I could even get in. . . ."

"You could," she says firmly, but he shakes his head.

"I'm not you."

"I don't exactly have a career picked out, either," Clare points out. "I have *no* idea what I want to do. I spent the last four years trying to get into college. I never really thought about what would come after that. I can't even decide on a major."

Aidan rolls his eyes. "Who has a major picked out before they ever set foot on campus? You're putting way too much pressure on yourself. It's totally normal not to know what you want to do with the rest of your life."

"Yeah, but I don't want to be normal. I want to know where I'm going."

"Maybe it's okay to be a little lost," he says, and even in the dark, she can see his eyes, round as the moon and focused entirely on her. "Especially when it's you."

"What does that mean?"

He shrugs. "Just that you can do anything. And you will. You've got all the time in the world to figure it out. But me?" He sweeps an arm out across the town, the quiet shops and the empty streets. "Honestly, this kind of thing is probably more my speed. And I'm okay with that. Maybe I'll coach." He holds up a half-eaten chocolate bar. "Or I'll open a candy shop. Or *garden*. I could always sell gardening tools."

Clare tries to imagine it: a future here in this town, the

same place where she grew up. But it's too hard to stretch her mind that far; there are so many things still to come before all that. Right now, the world feels huge and full of possibility, and if she ever returns to this tiny corner of it, she knows it will have to be after she's collected a whole slew of stories and memories and other experiences to bring back with her.

She reaches for Aidan's hand. "You're gonna do great things, too," she tells him. "You just don't know what they are yet."

He doesn't say anything, but his fingers close around hers, and Clare's heart sinks. Because right here—right now—it seems like an impossible thing: being with someone for any great length of time. It's crazy enough to imagine that what you look for in a person at seventeen might be the same at eighteen and nineteen and twenty. But to imagine you might be with the same person at seventeen as at twenty-seven—and then thirty-seven and forty-seven— seems like a leap of faith that borders on insane.

"So what's next, then?" Aidan asks, and Clare takes a deep breath.

"I don't know," she says, looking over at him. "Maybe we shouldn't worry so much about the future. It's not like there's any way to tell what's gonna happen that far down the road. We could end up almost anywhere . . . ." She pauses, considering her next words carefully. "But the one thing we know for sure is where we're gonna end up tomorrow. I'm going to New Hampshire and you're going to California. For four whole years. And whether we like it or not, we have to figure out what to do about that."

Aidan is watching her with a slightly bewildered expression. "I only meant..." he says, then gives his head a little shake. "I meant what's next *on the list*."

"Oh," Clare says, her face going hot. "Yeah. The list."

"But you're right," he says. "I know you're right. We need to figure this out."

They lock eyes, each waiting for the other to begin. Across the street, there's laughter as a group leaves Slices, and elsewhere, a far-off engine roars to life. Clare kicks nervously at the side of the fountain, letting her heels bounce off the stone, and Aidan blinks at her a few times.

"Okay," she says.

He nods. "Okay."

But still, it takes a few more seconds before she feels ready to start.

"Here's the thing," she says, before trailing off again, already stuck.

"Right," Aidan says. "The thing."

Clare takes a deep breath. "The thing is...if we stay together, I'm worried we'll be missing out on a lot of college stuff," she says, unable to look at him. "We're supposed to be throwing ourselves into it, but how can we possibly do that if we're always wishing we were somewhere else?"

"I know."

"And it means we'd always be missing—"

"I know," he says again, cutting her off, though not unkindly.

"And it would be impossible to—"

"It would," he agrees.

"But it's so hard to think about *not* being with you, either," she admits. "I hate the idea of waking up in a dorm room a few days from now and knowing that you're all the way on the other side of the country, but not knowing anything else. I don't want to wonder what you're doing, or what you're eating, or who you're meeting.... I can't stand the thought of not having any idea what's going on in your life. It's just too awful."

Aidan nods. "I feel the same way."

"We've hardly gone a day without seeing each other in two years," Clare says, staring at her hands. "I mean... you've been the most important person in my life."

"You too," he says, slipping an arm around her waist, and she leans against him, tucking herself into the familiar crook between his shoulder and his side.

"I don't want to let you go," she admits, and as she does, she realizes just how true it is. She can't imagine driving away tomorrow without knowing she can call him a hundred times from the road, meeting her roommate without texting him about it, starting her classes without a good-luck e-mail from him.

She can't imagine going about her days without Aidan to bear witness to them.

However much she knows that it's the right thing to do.

It's not until he runs his thumb gently across her cheek, wiping away a tear, that she realizes she's crying. She presses her face into the worn fabric of his shirt, listening to the thump of his heart, feeling the steady rise and fall of his chest.

After a few minutes have passed, he kisses the top of her head.

"It's over," he says, his voice breaking a little on the word. "Isn't it?"

She doesn't answer. She doesn't have to. They both know it's true. There's nothing to do now but nod into his shirt, trace the veins on the back of his hand, tip her head back and kiss him, long and hard and true, and then stand up together to leave this place behind, and start moving ahead to whatever comes next.

But just before they do, Aidan pauses to pull a penny from his pocket. He stands there a moment, rattling it in his palm, then tosses it into the fountain, where it makes a satisfying *plunk* before sinking to the bottom to join the constellation of other coins.

Clare is about to ask him what he wished for, but she stops herself.

She's pretty sure she already knows.

As they walk away, she glances back at the rippling water, trying not to think about the fact that instead of finding a souvenir here—something to carry forward with them—they've managed to leave something behind.

It breaks her heart a little.

STOP #8

The Party

11:11 PM

From the front porch of Andy Kimball's house, the music comes thumping through the windows with a force that makes the floorboards vibrate. Clare winces at the sound of it, already weary at the thought of what will greet them on the other side of the green door. She'd been tempted to go home after her talk with Aidan. But when she checked her phone on their way back to the car, there was a text from Stella, letting her know about the party—the last big bash thrown by someone from their class before everyone scattered to the wind—and it seemed to Clare a kind of a peace offering, one that she hadn't had the heart to refuse.

"I didn't realize so many people were still around," Aidan says, rising onto his toes to look through a window.

Watching him, Clare can't help thinking about all the other times they've stood here, on the threshold of so many parties just like this one. Ever since Andy's parents came into some money from her grandfather a few years ago and started traveling constantly, she could always be relied upon to throw a party. Especially when there was nothing else going on in this town, which was most of the time.

Clare can't imagine being fearless enough to give her house over to the masses so often, but she admires Andy for her creativity in explaining away a thousand broken vases over the years, wriggling out of countless warnings from the cops, and dodging blame for the many empty bottles in her parents' liquor cabinet.

"I think it's a lot of underclassmen," Clare says as Aidan steps back from the window with a frown.

"Where's Andy going again?"

"Michigan, maybe?"

He nods. "Right."

Though the porch isn't very big, they're standing a good three feet apart, and there's something odd about being so far away from him. They've never been the kind of couple who are all over each other, holding hands and making out in public; they're more private than that, more contained. But at this point, they've been together so long that being near him is a kind of habit; in some ways, Aidan feels more like an extension of herself than a whole other person.

Which is why neither of them ever really notices when Clare rests a hand on his arm while he's talking, or when Aidan hooks a foot around hers when they're sitting in a booth. Stella's always teasing them for the way they walk, so close together they tend to bounce off each other like a couple of bumper cars. And they're rarely more than a few feet away from each other at parties, as if held fast by some magnetic force.

But this is the type of closeness you don't notice until it's gone, until you're standing on opposite ends of a dimly lit porch less than an hour after deciding to break up, and all that's left between you is a vast and painfully polite distance.

"So," Aidan says, his face carefully neutral, "are we telling people?"

Clare looks up at him with alarm. She hadn't thought that far ahead yet.

"Sorry," he says, seeming a bit unnerved himself. "I just assumed..."

She shakes her head. "No, you're right. We probably should."

"Are you okay?"

"Yeah," she says, attempting a smile. "It's just kind of weird to be doing this."

He shifts as if to take a step toward her, then changes his mind and stays put. "I know," he says. "I wish we didn't..."

"Yeah," she says, once he trails off. "Me too."

They don't even bother knocking. There's no way anyone would hear it. Instead, Aidan pushes open the door, and the music blasts out into the quiet front yard, all rhythm and bass. When they step inside, they're met by a wall of heat and bodies, the foyer crowded with people holding red cups above their heads, some of them dancing, others talking, most just trying to get through.

121

"Why is it so crowded?" Aidan yells back to Clare, making a face. "I think I'm too old for this kind of thing."

"Good luck at college," she says, giving him a friendly pat on the shoulder.

"I'm gonna go get a drink. You want one?"

"Yeah, and if you see Stella..."

"Yeah?"

Clare hesitates, then shakes her head. "Never mind."

As he walks away, the top of his reddish hair visible above the crowd, Clare is struck by a completely illogical fear of losing sight of him. She watches as he pauses in the doorway between the foyer and the kitchen, bending a little as some girl, a junior on the girls' lacrosse team, leans close to say something to him. Clare's surprised by the stab of jealousy she feels at the sight, and she realizes this is how it will be from now on: next week and next month and next year.

Out in California, Aidan will soon be offering to get someone else a drink. Most likely someone tall and blond and impossibly beautiful, the kind of girl who gets asked whether she's a model even when she's doing something decidedly un-model-like, like eating chili fries or blowing her nose. Not long from now, it'll be someone else's hand he takes as they walk through a crowd, someone else he'll be cracking jokes with, telling stories to, huddling with in a corner at a thousand different parties.

Because he's no longer Clare's. And she's no longer his.

The thought wrenches at something inside her, makes

her knees go a little wobbly as she leans back against the blue wallpaper in the foyer.

She tries to force her mind in a different direction, far from California, all the way over to New Hampshire, where in spite of everything she's feeling at the moment, and in spite of how difficult it is to imagine from where she's standing right now, it's possible that there could be someone else waiting for her, too.

It might even be someone better—at least in theory— someone more suited to her than Aidan: the kind of guy who keeps a list of all the books he can't wait to read, who likes to watch something other than sports, who thinks a color-coded calendar system is kind of brilliant.

After all, it's not like she and Aidan have ever been perfect. They've never even been all that logical, in some ways. There are almost certainly better matches for both of them out there somewhere. So maybe this is just the way their story is supposed to go. Maybe, like her parents, this was all just a mistake they needed to make on their way to finding the one.

Maybe.

But that doesn't make it any easier.

A new song comes on over the speakers, and Clare pushes off from the wall, rising onto her tiptoes and looking toward the kitchen. She's debating whether to go find Aidan—who has yet to return with her drink, whether because he's still talking to that girl or because he forgot about it entirely; she isn't sure she wants to know—when someone puts a hand on her elbow. She turns to find one of their classmates, Anjali, smiling up at her.

"Hey," she says, holding up her cup for a toast, but she lowers it again when she realizes Clare doesn't have one. "When do you take off?"

"Tomorrow," Clare tells her. "You?"

"Not till next weekend, actually. Yale starts on the later side. I think I might be the last man standing."

Reflexively, Clare glances toward the doorway where Aidan disappeared. "You excited?" she asks, forcing herself to turn back to Anjali.

"Totally," she says. "And you know how I swore I'd never take math again after a whole year with Mr. Mitchell? Well, I actually got into this special economics program, so it looks like it's more statistics for me. What about you? Have you figured out your major yet?"

"Uh, we don't have to declare until sophomore year," Clare says distractedly as someone pushes past her. She presses her back up against the wall. "Lucky for me."

"Same with Yale, but I feel like most people already sort of know what they want."

"Well, not me," Clare says a little too brightly. "I still have no clue."

"Oh, come on," Anjali says with an encouraging smile. They're the same type of person, cut from the same mold. They've been in all the same honors classes for as long as Clare can remember, have gone head-to-head in GPA rankings, and have worked alongside each other at countless bake sales and soup kitchens and student council meetings. They've spent all of high school working hard and making plans, and now they're supposed to go off to college and jump headlong into whatever comes next.

Only Clare has no idea what that is yet.

"You're gonna have a million options," Anjali is saying, but Clare just stares at her.

"I don't know," she says. The room suddenly feels much too warm, and she wipes at her forehead. "I don't . . . everything's really up in the air right now. I guess . . ."

Anjali is watching her expectantly.

"I guess I'm just feeling a little lost."

"Oh," Anjali says, clearly surprised. "Well, that's okay."

"Do you mind if I . . . ?" Clare pauses to lick her lips. "Sorry, I just . . ."

Anjali steps aside to let her pass. "Sure, yeah. Of course. Good luck with everything if I don't see you."

The bathroom is just at the other end of the foyer, and after pushing her way through a group of underclassmen huddled around a video that's playing on someone's phone, Clare's relieved to find that it's empty. Someone has left a red cup on the sink, and the roll of toilet paper is unraveled on the tile floor, but otherwise, it's not in bad shape for a party like this.

The idea was just to escape, but she realizes now she actually has to go, and when she's done, she splashes some cold water on her face, then pauses to study herself in the mirror. It's about eleven thirty now, but it feels much later, and she realizes how exhausted she is. It seems like a million years ago that she told Aidan there would be no sleeping tonight, that they only had so much time left, and they had to make it count. Now, all she wants to do is curl up and go to bed.

When she opens the bathroom door, she's surprised to find the foyer is nearly empty now. But there's cheering coming from the direction of the backyard. She hurries through the kitchen, where a few people—unbothered by the commotion—are still sitting around the table playing cards, and then out past the living room and onto the patio, where the rest of the party seems to be bunched into a loose, shifting circle.

From where she's standing, a few feet back, Clare can tell it's a fight—the heavy *thwack* of landed punches, the jeering and shouting, the scraping of sneakers—but it's not until she pushes her way through the huddle that she realizes, with a shock, that it's Aidan and Scotty.

Aidan's head is low; he's got Scotty tucked in a headlock with one arm, and he's using the other to pummel him. It almost looks to Clare like they're just messing around, the way they so often do, and for a half second she lets herself believe it's true. But then she sees Scotty's face, which is red and distorted, and Aidan's, his teeth gritted and the vein on his forehead standing out.

As she watches in horror, Scotty twists free, swinging out and landing a punch squarely across Aidan's cheek. The smacking sound it makes, bone-crunching and solid, sets her heart racing. But Aidan barely reacts; he rocks back on his heels, then lurches forward again, landing a punch that cracks the side of Scotty's glasses.

Around them, everyone is shouting, though it's hard to tell whether they're egging them on or trying to get them to stop. Clare catches a quick glimpse of Stella's panicked face on the other side of the circle, her eyes flashing in the yellow light that's spilling out from the kitchen. And then Scotty takes another swing, and before she can think better of it, Clare's moving in their direction.

"Aidan," she shouts as she comes up behind him, but he doesn't respond. He doesn't even look at her. He's too busy staggering toward Scotty again. But Clare charges forward anyway, skidding to a stop right behind Aidan and reaching out to grab his arm, determined to end this before it can get any worse.

He shakes her off without even turning in her direction, his entire focus on Scotty, and so on her second try, Clare—still shouting for him to stop, determined to make him listen, though he's so clearly unable or unwilling to hear her—loops both arms around his waist in a kind of backward bear hug, then yanks back hard.

Her only thought is to get him out and away, to break them up before one of them gets seriously hurt, but everything is dark and blurry and confused, and just as she starts to tug on him, a bright flare of pain explodes above her right cheek, and she stumbles backward in shock, her hands cupped around her eye.

There are a few seconds when nobody reacts; Aidan and Scotty stop to stare at her, and the rest of the crowd looks on dumbly, as if they've forgotten they're not watching this on a screen, that they're here and now and part of this, too. It's so quiet they can hear the neighbor's dog barking to go out, a car pulling into the driveway, the sound of glassed-in laughter from the living room.

But then the moment snaps, and everything happens fast.

Even before Clare can fully register what happened— that she got popped in the eye, either by Scotty's fist or else Aidan's elbow, it's hard to know—Stella is there, taking her by the arm and leading her toward the kitchen.

Behind her, she can hear a flurry of panicked and excited voices, but above all the rest of them, Aidan and Scotty are shouting at each other.

"It was *you*," Aidan yells, his voice filled with fury.

"Was *not*," Scotty growls back at him, and then a few other people chime in, breaking them up yet again.

By the time they reach the kitchen, which Andy is busy clearing of people, Aidan and Scotty have trailed in behind Clare, their eyes full of worry as they hurry to her side, apologizing again and again.

"Get *back*," Stella snaps at them as she guides Clare over to a chair at the blocky wooden table—still strewn with cards from an abandoned game—and they obey. Aidan retreats to the doorway just behind Clare, so that she can't see him, and Scotty sinks miserably into a chair across from her, gingerly removing his broken glasses.

She can see now that one of his eyes is pink and puffy, his lip split wide open, and she twists to see if Aidan is hurt, too, but when she does, she feels the pain flare again behind her own eye, and Stella puts a hand on her shoulder, steadying her. Clare tries to mumble a few words of thanks, but Stella just shakes her head.

"Don't move," she says, then looks up at Andy, who is busy rooting around in the freezer. "Can you please hurry up?"

"There are no peas," she calls out, looking only vaguely concerned about the situation at hand. She's thrown enough parties to have dealt with just about everything, and this is not the first fight that's happened here by a long shot.

"Any steaks?" Scotty asks.

"No," Andy says, holding up a frozen pizza box. "Just this."

Stella rolls her eyes and crosses the space from the table to the fridge in three long strides. "Regular ice cubes are fine," she says, grabbing a bag of cups from the counter and dumping out the contents.

When she returns with the bag of ice, Clare still has a hand clapped firmly over her eye, which feels huge and bulging, like her palm is the only thing holding it in place. The whole side of her face is throbbing, and her eyelid feels thick and gluey, but she only registers all this in a distant way, numb and detached. She's still too shocked to be truly in pain.

"Don't I get one?" Scotty asks, pointing to the ice bag, and Stella glares at him as she drops into the seat beside Clare.

"I'm taking care of your collateral damage first."

"I'm so sorry," Scotty says to Clare for the millionth time, still shaking his head. "So, so, so sorry. We would have never—"

"Here," Stella says, ignoring him as she gently pries Clare's hand away from her face, replacing it with the ice pack, which stings at first, then—as she lets it settle there—starts to feel wonderfully cool, slowing the pulse that has sprung up somewhere behind her sore eye. "How does it feel?"

"Fine," Clare says, distracted. She turns to look at Aidan, who is slumped against the doorway, his hands in his pockets. He looks utterly miserable, and not just because of the cut below his right eye, which is raw and red. "What the hell were you guys thinking?" she says to him, then glances back at Scotty, who's wearing a slightly vacant expression.

"I don't know," he says, bringing two fingers to his lip and coming away with blood. He looks around for Andy, who seems to have drifted off, then reaches behind him for a napkin, dabbing at the cut. "It was stupid...."

"You think?" Stella asks, raising an eyebrow.

Aidan steps around so that Clare can finally see him with her one good eye. "You know that I'd never..." he says, his voice desperate and strained. He scrubs at his face with his hands, and she can see that one of his knuckles is split open. There's blood smudged across his fingers. "I'm sorry. I'm just...I feel terrible." He brings a hand to his chest, looking pained. "I hate the thought that something we did—"

"You did," Scotty says from across the table, still mopping at his lip with a napkin. "Something *you* did."

"You started it," Aidan says weakly.

"No way, dude," Scotty says, shaking his head. "I was just joking around about your sister. Which, by the way, you've got to lighten up about. But you were the one who threw the first punch."

Aidan flexes his jaw, but says nothing.

"And it wasn't me who clocked you," Scotty continues, his eyes moving to Clare. "I'm pretty sure it was Aidan's elbow."

"That's not the point," Clare says, feeling Aidan's gaze on her. She lowers the ice, but when she catches Stella's grimace at the sight of her eye, she shifts it back onto her cheek. "You guys are idiots for fighting at all."

"It *is* the point," Scotty says, sitting forward. "Because everyone's always blaming me for everything, and I'm always the screwup around here. But it wasn't me this time. It was your hothead boyfriend."

Nobody says anything, and Clare looks over at Aidan, a move that requires her to turn her whole head. His left eye is nearly swollen shut now, but the rest of his face is completely ashen, and his mouth has fallen half-open.

He looks like someone has punched him all over again.

They stare at each other, weighing something invisible

to the rest of the world, and then, finally, Clare tips her chin down.

"I'm not her boyfriend anymore," Aidan says quietly, still watching Clare, and after a pause, she nods in agreement.

"He's not my boyfriend anymore," she echoes, but something about the way they're saying it doesn't make it sound quite real.

She sets the dripping bag of ice on the table, scattering a few of the cards, and forces herself to look at Stella, who is staring at her, wide-eyed and genuinely astonished.

"Wow," she says, blinking a few times. "I'm gobsmacked."

Clare can't help smiling, though it makes her eye begin to throb again. "See? And you didn't think you'd get to use it today."

"There's no other word for it."

"You guys broke up?" Scotty says, looking from Aidan to Clare, then falling back into his chair. "I didn't think you'd actually ever do it."

Me neither, Clare thinks, trying to swallow the lump in her throat.

Beside her, Stella shakes her head in disbelief. "End of an era," she says, a little wistfully, and Clare glances over at Aidan, who attempts a smile in spite of his sore eye.

"End of an era," he echoes, and in spite of her sore heart, she smiles back at him, too.

STOP #9

The Dance

12:02 AM

Later, after the ice has melted and new bags have been made, after cuts have been cleaned and bandages pressed on, after the kitchen fills up again and the party resumes as if nothing ever happened, Aidan and Clare slip out to the empty patio together.

When they reach the spot where the fight occurred, they both stop. In the light from the kitchen windows, they can see a few drops of blood on the flagstones, and a small glinting sliver from Scotty's broken glasses.

"Scene of the crime," Aidan says, lifting his gaze. Stella fashioned him a thin white bandage out of some tape and gauze, and it sits just below his eye so that from a certain angle, it almost makes him look like a football player, or like one of those tourists with a needlessly thick layer of sunscreen.

But beneath all that, even in the shadows, Clare can see the regret scrawled across his face.

He scratches the back of his neck. "I really am sorry, you know."

"I know," she says. "I do. But I still don't get it. What the hell happened?"

"I don't know," he says with a shrug.

"This can't just be about your sister. That was over a year ago. And honestly, it wasn't even that bad. There's no way you can still be mad about it...."

He's doing his best to avoid her eyes, so Clare takes a step closer, putting an arm on each of his shoulders, forcing him to look at her.

"So what are you so upset about?"

"I don't know," he mumbles. "You and me, I guess. Tonight. Everything."

"Yeah, but those aren't reasons to use Scotty as a punching bag. You've been annoyed with him all night. How come?"

Aidan ducks away from her grip, walking to the edge of the deck, where he stands looking out over the yard. "I don't know," he says again, and when Clare walks over to join him, he sits down on the top step. "We used to always talk about California. Hanging out on the beach. Learning to surf. And now he's staying here."

"Yeah, but that's not—"

"It would've been so easy, you know?" Aidan says, the words tumbling out in a rush now. "All he had to do was go to class more often. Read a book every now and then. Pay attention. He's not an idiot. I mean, he is—but not in that way. All he had to do was try a little harder, and we could've been out there together."

Clare swallows hard, hurt by the truth of it: that she'd wasted so much time thinking similar thoughts about Aidan and Harvard, daydreaming about the two of them together on the East Coast. While all that time, Aidan was wishing the same thing—only about Scotty.

"I don't know," he says, kicking at the stones of the patio and scattering a few acorns. "I guess I didn't even realize I was pissed at him."

"You're not really," Clare says, her face growing warm as she thinks about her own conversation with Stella earlier. "You're just sad to leave. And you're taking it out on him."

Aidan shrugs. "It's just that so much is about to change. It'd be nice if there was at least one thing that could stay the same, you know?"

It takes Clare a moment to find her voice. "I know. But then..."

"What?"

"Well, how can you blame me for the Harvard thing?"

He furrows his brow. "What do you mean?"

"You were worried I'd want you to go," she says. "If you got in. And honestly, you might be right. I don't know. Sometimes it seems like it would be crazy to do anything other than break up. But other times..."

"Not so much."

"Not so much," she agrees. "Part of me still thinks it might've been nice to be closer."

135

Aidan bends to pick up an acorn, twisting at the little cap. "I know I should've told you."

"It's okay," she says, though it's not quite—at least not yet.

"But a lot of it was just that I felt really bad about the whole Stanford thing."

"I wasn't ever actually gonna—"

"I know," he says. "But still. I feel like we kind of had a deal, even if it was mostly just a joke. Even if neither of us expected it to go anywhere. But I just couldn't bring myself to do it. I couldn't pull the trigger on that stupid application."

"Because you were afraid I'd want you to go."

"No," he says, shaking his head. "Because I was afraid *I'd* want to go."

Clare looks at him sharply. "What?"

He shrugs. "I've always hated the idea of Harvard. Obviously. And you know I've always wanted to be in California. I mean, I still can't believe I got into UCLA...."

"I know, but—"

He cuts her off, looking down at the acorn in his palm. "But I was worried that if I got in, I might still choose Harvard."

"Why?"

"Because it would've been closer to you."

Clare stares at him. "Seriously?"

"I love you," he says simply, as if this is what she was asking. And she supposes that, in a way, it was.

"Aidan..." she begins, not sure what to say.

"I guess it doesn't matter now," he says. "I think we're both ending up in the right places. All of us, really. Maybe even Scotty. Who knows, right?"

She manages a nod. "Who knows."

Inside the house, the music has been turned up again, and people are streaming in and out of the kitchen with their cups held high, swaying to the beat.

Clare glances up at the sky, which is pocked with stars, and closes her eyes.

When she opens them again, Aidan is watching her intently, his face only inches from hers, as if he's about to kiss her. She pulls back uncertainly, and he frowns.

"You're definitely gonna have a shiner."

Clare brings a hand to her cheek, touching it lightly. "So are you," she says. "Maybe even two."

"Yeah, but on your first day at school..." he says with a groan. "I'm so sorry. I can't believe we did that."

"It's okay," she says, doing her best to smile in spite of the pressure of her swollen eye. "I'll look tough. No one'll want to mess with me."

He laughs. "Oh, yeah, you'll be super intimidating."

Behind them, someone slides open the screen door and then, with a burst of laughter, tosses a pair of sneakers out onto the patio. One of the shoes rolls over a few times and lands right behind them, and Aidan looks at Clare with a wrinkled nose.

"Does that smell like...?" he asks, and she nods.

"Puke. Definitely puke." She narrows her eyes at the damp sneaker. "Any chance you want to go for a walk or something?"

Aidan hops to his feet and extends a hand to help her up, too. "Let's get out of here."

Around the side of the house, there's a gated wooden fence that leads out to the street, which is still lined with cars, the sure sign of a successful party. When they pass Aidan's Volvo, Clare has an urge to climb in, to tell him to start the engine and just drive until they're somewhere, anywhere but California or New Hampshire. But instead, they walk past it without a word and continue down the street in no particular direction.

It's after midnight now, and the houses are mostly dark. Every once in a while, they see a flickering TV or the glowing eyes of a cat in a window, but for the most part, this area of town has already been tucked in, and the quiet is thick and ringing, a sound like static.

"I feel bad about your list," Aidan says after they've walked for a little while, turning right here and left there, winding their way deeper into the muffled suburban night. "I feel like it all sort of went awry."

Clare shrugs. "That's what I get for over-planning."

"What did we skip?"

The slip of paper is in her pocket, but she doesn't take it out. "I don't know. We were supposed to get ice cream. Stop by the movie theater. Go to the gazebo."

"Those weren't firsts, though, right?"

"No, just places that meant something."

"I'm sorry we didn't make it, then," he says, looking at her sideways, and the words flood Clare with a kind of icy grief. She stops walking without meaning to and stares at him, and when Aidan turns around, she can see the recognition on his face, can see the look behind his eyes as he realizes exactly what he just said.

"Oh," he says quietly. "I didn't mean it like that."

Clare swallows hard. "I know."

"But I am."

"What?"

"Sorry we didn't make it."

"Me too," she says, and then they begin to walk again, a little bit closer this time.

"So where were we supposed to be right now?"

At first, it seems to Clare that this, too, might be some larger question with a deeper meaning.

They're supposed to be on a deserted island.

They're supposed to be at the same college.

They're supposed to be together.

But then she realizes he's talking about the list.

"I don't know. The dance, I think. But we already ruled that one out."

Aidan stops walking and turns to face her. "Am I allowed to be romantic now?"

"Now that we've broken up?"

He laughs. "Yeah."

Without waiting for an answer, he steps forward, circling his arms around her waist, pulling her close, and she automatically clasps her hands at the back of his neck and leans into him, as she's done so many times before.

They don't move—not really. It's more of a hug than a dance, the two of them standing there in the dark, locked together like they're afraid to let go. She can smell the antiseptic that Stella used on his cut, a clean, tangy scent, and beneath that, the peppermint shampoo his mother bought for him. She traces a finger along his back, just between his shoulder blades, and she feels him shiver beneath her touch. When he bends to kiss her temple, it makes her feel like crying.

"Remember that night?" she asks, and she's surprised to hear her voice tremble a little bit. "You kept spilling punch all over yourself."

He bows his head, laughing softly into her ear. "I was nervous."

"You were a mess."

"But a charming mess."

"You were holding your cup while you danced," she says, pressing her cheek against his chest. "It was sloshing all over the place. But you refused to put it down."

"I needed something to do with my hands," he admits. "I was afraid you'd see what a terrible dancer I am. I needed a diversion."

"So you sacrificed your suit."

"It was for a very worthy cause."

They hadn't been anything official yet, that night: just two people who liked each other, on the brink of something more. But already, she was beginning to see what it might be like, being with Aidan. Around them, everything else felt plodding and predictable, their classmates all going through the motions, carrying out the overly dramatic business of every school dance: the girls crying in the bathroom, the couples making out in the corners, the two groups of guys on the cusp of a fight, the upperclassmen practicing their most withering stares.

But Aidan—Aidan was *fun*. All night, he'd danced around her: moonwalking and then break-dancing, marching them around in a stiff-armed tango and then reeling her back for a comically formal waltz, spinning and swinging her so quickly she could hardly see straight. He was nervous and jittery, but also whirling and unpredictable, with flashing eyes and a dazzling smile that was only for her. She was laughing so hard she could barely keep up, and she kept having to stop and catch her breath.

"I've got two left feet," he'd shouted to her over the music, his face flushed in the heat of the gym, "but I know how to use them."

There was just something about him. He made the room feel brighter and the hours move faster. All that night, they were flying, and it was like magic, giddy and joyful and dizzying.

But even so, there was a part of her that wished he might

slow down. Just for a little while, just long enough for her to walk into his arms and fit herself against him, to stand there while the minutes ticked by, just holding him in place, this one bright spot in the midst of so much gray.

And now, two years later, they're finally here: folded together like this, with the night thrumming all around them and the sound of his heartbeat loud in her ears.

And yet, he's no longer hers.

All this, and the only thing it means is goodbye.

They stand there like that for a long time, so long she starts to think she can feel each minute slipping away as the night hurtles unrelentingly toward morning. But then Aidan goes abruptly tense, and he loosens his grip, letting her go and taking a step back.

"I'm sorry," he says, and she can see the change in his eyes, the sudden recollection of what they are to each other now—or rather, what they're not. "I guess I just don't know how to do this yet."

Clare feels a little unsteady. "Do what?"

"Not be together."

"Oh," she says. "Yeah. I know." Her phone makes a whirring noise from her bag, and she glances down at it, then back up at Aidan. "It'll probably be a lot easier when we're apart."

There's a wounded expression on his bruised face.

"Sorry," she says as her phone goes off again. She fumbles through her bag until she finds it. "I didn't mean it like that. I just think it'll get better when we're not together."

She groans, then shakes her head. "Sorry. That didn't come out right, either."

His face softens. "It's okay. We're still new at this."

"Yeah," she says, holding up the blue-lit screen of her phone as proof. The electronic numbers across the front read 12:24 AM. "It's only been a couple hours."

"Then we've still got time to practice," he says, rubbing his hands together. "What should we do now? I guess it's too late to cover the stuff we missed, but we could still try to hit whatever's next on the list...." He trails off when he sees that she's not listening. She's too busy staring at the long chain of missed calls and texts on her phone. "Clare?"

She looks up at him, her eyes wide. "Uh, the next stop isn't on the list, actually," she says. "Unless you have some sort of record I don't know about."

He stares at her, confused. "Record?"

"Come on," she says, already turning in the direction of the car. "We've got to go to the police station."

"What?" Aidan asks, jogging after her. "*Why?*"

"Because," she tells him. "Scotty's in jail."

STOP # 10

The Police Station

12:44 AM

When she comes flying through the front doors of the police station, the first thing Clare sees is Stella. She's sitting hunched in one of three blue plastic chairs opposite the main desk, staring vacantly at the dirty floor and gnawing at one of her fingernails. And though it's after midnight and Clare has somehow found herself in the town's police station for the very first time in her life, it's this detail that shocks her the most.

Stella doesn't bite her nails. She isn't a person with nervous habits, because *nothing* makes her nervous. She's fearless and unwavering and bold. And her nails, like the rest of her, always look perfect, with dark polish to match the rest of her outfits. So seeing her like this now is a little bit alarming.

"Hey," Clare says gently, sliding into the chair beside her. "You okay? What's happening? Where is he?"

Stella seems surprised to see her, as if she's already forgotten that she asked them to come. She blinks at Clare, then lowers her hand and rubs at the jagged nail.

"I don't know," she says with a shrug. "They'd already taken him back when I got here, so I haven't seen him. Someone told me he'd be out pretty soon. So that must be a good sign, right?"

Aidan is standing on the far side of the room, trying to look through the window and past the empty desk to the back of the station for any sign of Scotty. Giving up, he finally turns and walks back to them. "What'd he do?"

"I don't know," Stella says, her eyes darting from Aidan to Clare. "We were kind of arguing, I guess, and he stormed out of Andy's—"

Aidan grunts, as if he should have expected as much, then resumes his pacing.

"And then, well, he must've gotten lost or something. . . ."

Clare raises her eyebrows. "Lost?"

"He fell asleep," Stella says, biting her lip.

"Where?" Aidan and Clare say at the exact same time.

"In a neighbor's flowerbeds. So they called the police."

"*Seriously?*" Aidan asks, coming to a stop, and Clare can see that he's trying not to laugh, though he's doing a terrible job of it. She presses her lips together, feeling the same way. She's not sure exactly what she'd imagined Scotty had been hauled in for, but this certainly wasn't it.

"I know," Stella says, shaking her head. "He's such an idiot." But the way she says it—so fondly, her eyes shining—makes Clare look at her harder, and when she does, Stella ducks her head to hide the fact that she's blushing.

Stella doesn't usually blush, either.

Before Clare can say anything, Aidan frowns. "So are they charging him with anything?"

"I don't know," Stella says. "They wouldn't tell me."

He gives her an odd look. "Wait...if you weren't with him, how did you know to come here?"

"He got one phone call..." she says, before trailing off.

"And he didn't call me?" Aidan asks, looking confused, but before Stella can respond, the door beside the desk is flung open, and for the second time tonight, Clare is surprised to see the round, merry face of Officer Lerner.

"Hi," she says, shooting up from the chair, relieved that it's not some random cop they'll be dealing with, but someone they actually know.

Officer Lerner's brow creases at the sight of her, but then she can see it register—who she is, why she's here—and he smiles, tapping his hand twice against a clipboard.

"So we meet again," he says. "I take it you're a friend of young Mr. Wright?" He glances down at his paperwork, and then—just as abruptly—his eyes fly back up to Clare's face. "Hey, are you..." he asks, his face darkening as he notices Aidan, too. "Are you okay?"

"I'm fine," she assures him. "Really. There was just... it's a really long story."

He takes a step closer, his head tilted to one side. "Boy, that's gonna be quite the shiner tomorrow," he says. "Are you sure—"

"Yup, totally fine," she says again, trying too hard to keep the impatience out of her voice. "Is Scotty okay?"

He takes off his hat and rubs at the shiny bald spot on the top of his head. Then his face reddens slightly, and Clare gets the distinct impression he's trying not to laugh. "Yeah, he's fine," he says. "We had a nice little chat about boundaries and responsibility and trespassing and underage drinking. But seeing as he's a first-time offender, and that it's everyone's last night in town, and he wasn't causing any real trouble, we agreed that a warning would be sufficient."

"That's great," Stella says, calmer already. "Does that mean... Will he be able to leave now?"

"Oh, yeah," Officer Lerner says, chuckling a little. "He'll be out in a minute. He's just... getting cleaned up a bit."

"Cleaned up?" Aidan asks, looking confused.

"Yeah. You guys keep an eye on him from now on, okay?" he says with a wink as he opens the door behind him. "And don't be getting into any more trouble tonight, you know? Tomorrow's a new beginning. You want to start it out right." He replaces his hat, then gives them a little wave. "Good luck with everything."

When he's gone, they all three exchange mystified looks. Clare is about to say something to Stella, but then the door bangs open again, and this time a younger officer appears, smirking and shaking his head.

Scotty is only about two steps behind him, and when he enters the lobby, he stops and bends in a deep bow. "Ladies," he says, looking from Stella to Clare, and then at Scotty. "Gentleman."

This is met by only silence as they stare at him, open-mouthed. He must have lost his T-shirt somewhere along the way, and he stands there now wearing only his low-slung jeans, his plaid boxers sticking out at the top, and his bare, skinny chest is completely covered in black finger-prints. On the side of his face, there's a dark black square that goes from the corner of his mouth all the way up to the place where a bruise is starting to bloom beneath his eye, as if he face-planted straight into an ink pad. He looks like something out of either a children's book or a horror story, like a piece of Swiss cheese, or maybe some kind of insane spotted animal.

"What the hell?" Aidan asks, his jaw still hanging.

The officer behind him is full-out laughing now. "He was disappointed that we've switched to electronic finger-printing."

"So I found the ink pad on one of the desks!" Scotty says proudly.

"*Really*," Clare says, trying not to laugh.

"Next time," the officer tells him, "maybe you should think twice about stealing anything from a police station."

Scotty turns around and salutes him. "Aye, aye, Captain."

"I already told you, I'm not a captain," the man says, rolling his eyes. He looks over at the rest of them. "You'll get him home?"

Aidan nods. "Thanks so much for being so understanding."

"That ink isn't coming off for a little while," the man says with a chuckle. "I think that's punishment enough."

Stella hasn't said a word yet. She's still just standing

there, staring at this swaying, staggering, polka-dotted version of Scotty. But as soon as the officer leaves, and it's just the four of them in the empty lobby, she takes a step forward, giving him a hard look.

"You could've been arrested," she says, thrusting a finger at him. "You could've been charged with something."

Scotty holds up both hands, which are smeared with black. "Yeah, but I wasn't."

"I know this night is hard for you," Stella says in a low voice, "but you can't do this kind of thing anymore. You just can't. We're not gonna be around to fix things for you after tonight, so it's time to grow up. You get that, right?"

The grin on Scotty's face disappears. "Hey," he says in a pleading tone, but she's not listening. She's already turned on her heel and is walking out of the building, letting the door slam shut behind her as she disappears into the darkened parking lot.

There are a few seconds of clanging silence, and when she turns back to Scotty, Clare sees that his arms are hanging limp at his sides. His broken glasses are balanced at an odd angle on his nose, and there's an injured expression on his battered, ink-stained face. She lets out a sigh.

"I'll go," she says. "Just give me a minute."

Outside, Stella is already halfway across the parking lot, which is still slick from the earlier rain. By the time Clare catches up with her, she's breathing hard.

"Hey," she says, grabbing her friend's arm, and Stella

whirls around. "Why are you so upset? I mean, it's Scotty. He does this stuff...."

Stella gives her a cool look. "I thought you were done caring about me."

"I never said that. I only said I have to stop needing you so much."

"Same thing."

"It's not, actually," Clare tells her. "And I wasn't trying to be mean. It's just...I don't know. You clearly can't be bothered to act like my friend anymore, so what else am I supposed to do?"

"God, you're doing it again," Stella says, tipping her head back with a groan. "Even now. You came out here to see why I'm upset, and now you're talking about yourself again."

Clare frowns at her. "What?"

"Have you ever considered the possibility that not everything is about you?" Stella asks, taking a step closer. "That maybe the big dramatic farewell between Clare Rafferty and Aidan Gallagher isn't the only thing going on tonight?"

"That's not fair."

"I'm sorry this is hard for you," Stella says with a shrug. "I am. But I'm also just so tired of talking about whether you and Aidan will break up or stay together, and who wants what, and why. It's exhausting."

"Well," Clare says, glaring at her now, "we broke up already, so I guess you're off the hook."

Stella's face softens, just slightly. "I know. And I'm sorry. But it's what you wanted, and you guys seem to be handling it just fine, so I don't know what else you want from me."

"I don't want anything from you."

"Yet you're so busy worrying about how I'm not paying enough attention to you," she says, "that you haven't even asked about *me*."

Clare throws her hands up. "Well, I don't get it. You're upset because Scotty's in jail, which makes no sense at all. I mean, you saw him. He looks like a drunken Dalmatian. What do you expect?"

To her surprise, Stella laughs at this.

"What?" Clare demands, kicking at the asphalt with the toe of her shoe.

"Nothing. It's just that I was thinking you look sort of like a raccoon, with your eye like that. Aidan, too."

Clare allows a small smile. "I guess we're all kind of a mess tonight."

They're both silent for a moment, studying their feet. A car pulls into the parking lot, the headlights scraping past them, illuminating their faces just briefly before leaving them once again in the dark.

"I still don't get it," Clare says after a moment.

Stella looks at her evenly. "So ask."

"Ask what?"

"Ask me why I'm upset. Ask me why I've been so busy. Ask me why things have felt different lately."

"I've been asking you that all night."

"No, you haven't. You've been asking me why I'm too

152

busy for *you*. Why I haven't been there for *you*. You haven't once asked where I've been."

"Fine," she says, a little impatiently. "So where *have* you been?"

Stella hesitates, then sighs. "Forget it."

"No, I want to know," Clare insists, but Stella is distracted by the clatter of a metal door, which echoes out across the parking lot. They both look over to see the boys come walking out the front of the station. Scotty is wearing Aidan's button-down, which is hanging open so that the paleness of his chest stands out against the inky spots, and Aidan is trailing behind him in only a white undershirt that's a little too small. They make a ridiculous pair as they stride over with matching grins.

When they reach Clare and Stella, Scotty produces a black marker, which he must have stolen as well, holding it out in front of him like a trophy. "Look," he says, laughing. "I'm a human game board. Who wants to play connect-the-dots?"

Aidan snatches the marker from him, hiding it behind his back. "Let's not make it worse," he says, and Stella rolls her eyes. She looks around at each of them in turn—Scotty with his polka dots, Aidan with a bright line of white tape across his cheek, Clare with her swollen eye—and shakes her head.

"I'm pretty sure," she says, turning to walk toward the car, "it can't get much worse than this."

STOP #11

The Wrights' House

1:24 AM

At Scotty's house, all the windows on the second floor are dark, which means his parents have already gone to sleep. This isn't usually a problem. Over the years, they've mastered the art of the after-hours entrance: tiptoeing and shushing and whispering on their way through the kitchen, where they usually grab a few snacks, and then heading out to the deck to drag the scattered lawn chairs into a circle and let the clock wind down on their curfews.

But tonight, Scotty is still keyed up from his brush with the law, and as they burst into the quiet kitchen, he trips over one of the barstools, stumbling a few steps before crashing into the hutch. The whole thing rattles and chimes, the delicate plates and glasses quivering on their shelves, and they all hold their breath until it settles again.

"Oops," Scotty whispers, once they're certain that his parents haven't woken up.

"Maybe I should make some coffee," Aidan suggests,

and Stella gives him a thumbs-up as she and Clare start steering Scotty out of the kitchen.

In the bathroom, they sit him on the closed seat of the toilet and then assess the damage with matching frowns. He looks back and forth at them, pushing his broken glasses up on his nose every few seconds, only to have them immediately slide down again.

"I'm not sure soap is gonna do it," Stella says eventually, and Clare nods from where she's leaning backward against the sink, doing her best to avoid the giant mirror above it. She isn't quite ready to see the damage to her own face just yet.

"I feel like we need bleach or something."

"Bleach?" Scotty repeats with a worried look.

"What else do you use for this kind of thing?" Stella asks, tapping her chin. "Turpentine? Nail polish remover?"

Scotty stares at his blackened palms, splaying his fingers. "Maybe it'll just go away on its own," he says hopefully. "I bet it might even be gone by morning."

"Sorry, pal," Clare says, shaking her head. "I think you're looking at a few really awkward days with those spots."

Scotty hides his face in his hands with a groan.

"Not to mention the black eye," Stella adds cheerfully. "All the girls at your new school will probably run away screaming."

"What about dish soap?" Clare suggests, and Scotty claps his inky hands.

"Brilliant," he says. "Isn't that what they use on the animals when there's an oil spill?"

"Are you seriously comparing your crazy finger-painting spree to the plight of a baby seal?" Stella asks with a raised eyebrow, and Scotty makes a face at her.

It's quick, so quick that Clare might have missed it if she'd looked away even for a second, but there's something about this exchange, this moment between them—silly as it is—that feels almost charged. They hold each other's eyes for a beat too long, and then, with a goofy grin, Scotty spins around and walks out the door to find the soap.

As soon as he's gone, Clare widens her eyes at Stella. "That's it," she says, trying to keep the surprise out of her voice.

"What, dish soap?"

"No. You and Scotty."

Stella pauses—just for an instant—in the middle of folding a towel, the corners still matched neatly at the edges. "Scotty," she says dismissively, "is an idiot."

"Yeah," Clare says, grinning now, "but he's your idiot."

Stella hangs the towel carefully on the silver bar near the sink, then turns around again with a wary look. "Okay, just say it," she says, and there's a challenge to her tone.

"Say what?"

"It's Scotty we're talking about here. So you must have some sort of opinion."

Clare hesitates. "I think it's... great."

"You do," Stella says flatly. It's not a question.

"I do. I mean...I'm surprised, obviously. You have to give me a minute to get my head around it."

Stella places both hands on the sink, rocking back and forth. "This is why I didn't want to tell you."

"What? No. Come on. I think it's great."

"You already said that."

"How long has it been going on?"

Stella straightens again. "A few weeks. Maybe a month."

"Wow," Clare says, failing to hide her astonishment. "And nobody knows?"

"Nope," she says with a faint smile. "Turns out, he's not always such a bigmouth."

There's a sound in the hallway, and they both freeze, listening for footsteps. But when it gets quiet again, Clare hoists herself up onto the sink.

"You and Scotty," she says, the idea of it still settling over her.

"It's not *that* crazy, is it?" Stella asks, absently ripping off a square of toilet paper. She begins to shred it into tiny pieces, which flutter like leaves onto the tiled floor.

For Clare, this is almost more of a shock than finding out about Scotty in the first place: Stella—who never cares what people think of her—seems to be nervously waiting for her approval.

"You really like him," she says, beginning to understand that this is more than what it seems, that perhaps it goes deeper than it might appear.

Stella drops the last bit of toilet paper, then wipes her hands on her jeans. "I don't know," she says, unable to meet Clare's eyes.

"You do," she says gently. "I can tell. And I don't think it's crazy at all."

Stella lets out a hoarse laugh. "It's a little crazy," she admits. "But there's just something about him. We've been fighting for so many years that I kind of forgot what it was about. And he's funny, you know? I mean, he drives me nuts, too, but..."

"But you like him."

She shrugs helplessly. "I like him."

Clare scoots over, patting the counter, and Stella hops up beside her so that their swaying feet drum in rhythm against the cabinet below. "I know I've been a self-involved jerk lately," she says, relieved to see Stella smile at this. "But I wish you would've told me."

"I know," she says, glancing down at her hands, which are folded in her lap.

"It's just that...if we can't even tell each other the big stuff now, while we're here together, how are we ever gonna survive being apart next year?"

"I know," Stella says again. "I guess I just wanted to see what happened with it first. I didn't realize it would turn into something more than just fun, and then when it did, I didn't know how everyone else would react. Especially you and Aidan."

"Well, Aidan will probably be relieved it isn't Riley."

Stella laughs. "Good point."

"And I actually really like the idea of you guys together," Clare says, leaning into her a little. "I think it's kind of perfect. For whatever that's worth."

"It's worth a lot," Stella says just as the door is nudged open again, and Scotty appears holding a half-filled container of green dish soap.

"What?" he asks, when they both go abruptly quiet. He brings a hand to the blocky stain on his cheek with a sigh. "It can't have gotten worse...."

"It's fine," Stella says, sliding off the counter and taking the soap from him. "It still looks like a tattoo gone horribly wrong. Sit down. We've got our work cut out for us."

Ten minutes, two towels, one roll of toilet paper, half a bottle of dish soap, and a whole lot of scrubbing later, they give up. As it turns out, the ink is even more stubborn than Scotty, and all their efforts hardly make a dent. There are still thumbprints all over him, not to mention the black square across his swollen face.

"It's fine," Scotty says miserably. "When we're getting to know each other, I'll just tell all my new friends that my mom is a ladybug and my dad's a leopard."

In the kitchen, Aidan is pouring steaming mugs of coffee, and they wrap their fingers—pruney from the soap and water—around them gratefully, then head outside, where the night is cool and still and winking with fireflies.

"So," Scotty says, once they're settled on the plastic

160

chairs, which they've pulled to the far side of the deck so they won't wake his parents, "I have a theory."

Aidan raises his eyebrows. "Yes?"

"I think I might—*might*—be having a harder time with this whole being-left-behind thing than I thought."

Stella laughs. "You think?"

"Side effects include spontaneous fisticuffs and severe ink-face," he says with a sheepish grin.

Beside Clare, Aidan clears his throat. "I guess..." he begins, then pauses, scratching at his chin, clearly working up to his own apology. Finally, he lifts his eyes to meet Scotty's. "I guess I might be having a harder time than I thought, too. With the whole you-being-left-behind thing."

Scotty smiles ruefully. "I know it wasn't supposed to be like this."

"Yeah," Aidan says. "But I've been kind of a jerk about it."

"Kind of?" Scotty asks, pointing at his fat lip.

"Okay, I've been a huge jerk."

"No more than usual," Scotty says with a grin, and then he shrugs. "It was always gonna be hard, right? Even if we were all in the same place next year, everything would still be different, and that sucks. But it's also kind of the point, I guess. New beginnings and all that..."

A quiet falls over them, and Clare stares at the slats of the deck, knowing that he's right. It's time to move on, and the more time they spend wishing it were otherwise, the harder it will be to let go.

"But I still hate that you're all leaving," Scotty says. "Seriously. It's the worst. And you're all the worst for doing it."

Clare lifts her mug. "We'll miss you, too," she says as everyone else follows suit.

"Cheers," Aidan says. "To us."

"To us," Stella echoes.

"But mostly to me," Scotty says, breaking the spell, and when they all give him an exasperated look, he shrugs. "What? I'm the one who's stuck here. I think we can all agree I need the most cheers out of anyone."

Stella crosses and then uncrosses her legs, studying his face with amusement. "Your parents are gonna *flip* when they see you tomorrow."

"I'll just tell them you did it," he jokes, but she only rolls her eyes.

"It can't be worse than the time we stole your dad's cigars," Aidan says. "Remember? We smoked them right out here...."

"And then we forgot to bring the rest inside, and there was that huge thunderstorm," Clare reminds them. "They were completely ruined."

"Yeah, my dad was pretty pissed about that one," Scotty says. "Though it wasn't as bad as the time me and Aidan left the sunroof open in the car."

"What, it rained?" Stella asks, and Scotty shakes his head.

"Snowed."

"Why in the world would you have the sunroof open in the—"

"Because," Aidan says, his eyes dancing, "Scotty wanted to try to catch a snowflake on his tongue while we were driving."

After that, the stories come thick and fast, punctuated by laughter and interrupted only by the occasional teasing. Above them, the stars burn brightly in the night sky, and the minutes continue to tick past as the four of them sit there trading memories and fighting off sleep, hoping that this might be enough to hold back the morning.

It isn't until later, once they've grown quiet again, once all the coffee is gone and the mugs are empty, that Stella tips herself off her lawn chair, struggling to her feet with a yawn. "I think I need more caffeine," she says as she stretches, and Clare offers to help.

In the kitchen, Stella pours the last inch of cold coffee into the sink, then grabs the canister from a shelf. There's something so deliberate in the way she moves around, navigating cabinets and drawers with ease; it's clear she's been spending a lot of time here.

"So are you okay?" Stella asks as she grabs a filter, and Clare shrugs.

"I'm a little tired, but I'm sure the coffee will help."

"No, I mean about Aidan."

"I thought you didn't want to hear about that."

Stella glances over her shoulder with an impatient look. "Of course I do. I was just upset before. So I said some things. And so did you. But it'll be a while before we see each other again, and I don't want to leave it like that. So tell me. Are you okay?"

"I don't know yet," Clare says, leaning back against the counter. "Do I seem okay?"

"Aside from the eye?"

Clare presses a finger to her cheek and winces. "Forgot about that for a second."

"Well, it's not gonna make it any easier to forget about Aidan."

"I think it was Scotty who got me, actually."

"Then I guess it won't be easy to forget about him, either," Stella says, hitting the start button and turning around. "I know it won't for me, anyway."

"Do you have to?" Clare asks. "I mean, can't you just…"

"See how it goes?" she asks, giving Clare a funny look. "Come on. This from the girl who put together a whole scavenger hunt to decide the fate of her relationship."

"It wasn't a scavenger hunt. Why does everyone keep calling it that?"

"Whatever," Stella says. "The point is…you needed an answer because you're leaving tomorrow." She glances down at her watch. "Today. You're leaving today. And so am I."

"Yeah, but if you really like him…"

"C'mon, Clare," Stella says, wiping her hands on a towel. "Listen to yourself. Why would it be different for

164

us? You and Aidan were together forever. This was just a summer thing. It wasn't ever meant to last."

"But do you want it to?"

Stella tilts her head back, gazing at the ceiling. "I'm not sure," she says. "But there are a lot of possibilities besides *stay together* and *break up*, you know. Not everything has to be so black-and-white."

"Says the girl who only wears black."

Stella laughs. "You know what I mean."

The smell of coffee fills the kitchen as it starts to brew, bitter and warm, and Clare closes her eyes, inhaling deeply. She thinks, for a moment, about all the things her parents have been telling her this summer. How college is the first chapter of the rest of your life. The beginning of everything. The place where you meet your lifelong friends.

Clare understands that this is supposed to be comforting. They're just trying to be enthusiastic, assuring her that the best is yet to come. But it feels like what they're saying is that everything she's done up until now isn't important enough to last. That all these years, all these memories— none of it actually counts. That it's all just going to disappear behind her like a trail of bread crumbs. And only she knows the truth: that without it, she'll be lost.

Besides, she already has a lifelong friend, and it's hard to imagine a better qualification for the title than having known someone forever.

She opens her eyes again. "I'm gonna miss this."

Stella gives her an odd look. "Making coffee together in Scotty's kitchen? I'm pretty sure we've never done this before."

"No," Clare says. "You."

"You'll be fine," Stella says. "We both will. Everyone says you make fast friends in college."

"I don't know," Clare says. "I think I prefer slow friends."

Stella smiles. "Me too."

"That better not be a crack about me," Scotty says, pushing open the screen door, and when his gaze lands on Stella, it lingers there. Watching him, watching them, Clare wonders how she hasn't seen it before, this new closeness between them. There's something reassuring about it, something that just seems to fit.

"I'll let you two finish up in here," she says, smiling at Stella as she steps around Scotty, slipping out the door before they can object.

Outside, she swats away the mosquitoes as she crosses the deck to find Aidan asleep on one of the lounge chairs, his head tipped to one side. Quietly, she lowers herself onto the chair beside him, lying curled on her side, so that when he jolts awake, it's to find her face only inches from his.

"No sleeping, remember?" she says, beaming at him.

He sits up, still drowsy. "Why do you look like that?"

"Like what?" she says, then points at her eye with a grin. "Oh, this? Probably because you punched me in the face."

"Not *that*," he says, giving her a weary look as he swings his feet to the ground. "Why do you look so...happy?"

"I don't know," she says honestly. "I guess I just missed you."

He frowns at her. "How long was I asleep?"

"Not long," she assures him.

Overhead, a plane flies past, and they track it across the sky, a little bead of light moving through the clouds, which are gauzy and gray against all the blackness. Clare sits up, facing Aidan so that their knees are touching in the space between the chairs.

"So was this on the list?"

She nods. "Any guesses?"

"First time I opened a door for you?"

She shakes her head.

"First time we played footsie?" he says, nudging at her sandaled foot with his own.

"Nope."

"First time I bought you a drink?"

"Very funny."

"First time I...sneezed on you?"

She laughs. "Maybe."

"First time you watched me throw up?"

"It's possible."

"First time I accidentally tripped you while walking behind you?"

"Wow," she says. "I never realized what a mess you are."

"Stop sweet-talking me," he says, laughing, then he holds up a finger in the direction of the giant chestnut tree that forms a canopy over the other end of the deck. "I know. The first time we saw that owl with the glasses up there."

"It wasn't wearing glasses, you clown," she says, shaking her head. "It just looked that way because it was so dark."

"I'm pretty sure I saw a pair of specs," he said. "But you believe whatever you want."

"I always do," she says as he flops back onto the chair.

"Okay, I give up. Just tell me."

Clare smiles. "It was the first time we talked all night."

"Oh, yeah," Aidan says, sitting up again.

"Remember how we completely lost track of time?"

"And we both got in trouble for breaking curfew."

"Yeah, but it was worth it."

Aidan glances up at the sky. "Can you believe there was ever a time when there was so much we didn't know about each other it filled up a whole night?"

Clare frowns. "What do you mean?"

"Just that...to spend a whole night talking with someone is kind of a big thing. There was still so much we were learning about each other then."

"You don't think we still have anything to learn?"

"Not like at the beginning," he says, swiping at a bug. "Not like we did then. But that's a good thing. You know me better than anyone in my life ever has. It's actually kind of crazy, when you think about it." His eyes catch hers in the dark, holding her gaze. "It's hard to imagine anyone else ever knowing me this well."

"But that's the thing," Clare says, looking away. "Somebody will. And then it'll seem crazy to you that you once thought nobody would ever know you as well as that random girl you dated in high school."

He smiles, a little sadly. "You'll never just be *that random girl I dated in high school*, you know. No matter what, even if we never talk to each other again, you're still part of my story now—a big part—and I'm a part of yours. There's no changing that."

"Yeah, but what if it's true, what everyone's been saying?"

Aidan gives her a questioning look.

"That our lives are only just beginning," Clare explains. "What if one day we look back on this, and it's just a hazy memory? What if you and me—all this—what if it's *not* a big part of our story? What if it's just the prologue?"

"Oh, come on," Aidan says. "The prologue is the best part. Everyone knows that."

"I guess."

"And you and me? We must be at *least* up to chapter four by now. Tonight alone has to be a whole chapter."

"You think?"

"It is for me."

"Me too," she says, and without thinking about it, she reaches out and takes his hand. He gives hers a little squeeze in return, and they remain there like that, sitting motionless on the edges of their chairs, their knotted hands dangling between them.

"You know why I picked Stanford?" she asks softly, and Aidan lifts his chin. "Because I knew I'd never get in."

He furrows his brow, confused.

"If I'd tried for somewhere easier on the West Coast, I was afraid that I might choose that, too."

Aidan's smile is slow to emerge. "You know the most ridiculous part of this whole thing? Stanford isn't actually anywhere near UCLA. And Harvard isn't all that close to Dartmouth, either."

"So you're saying I shouldn't major in geography?"

He laughs. "I'm saying we still would've had to drive hours to see each other. It still would've been a huge change. And it still would've been really hard."

"I'm glad we're both going where we want to go," she says, letting his hand drop. "I think it's the way it's supposed to be, you know?"

"I know," he says around a yawn, and Clare realizes her own eyelids are heavy, too.

"Coffee," she says, glancing behind her at the house. "Whatever happened to the coffee?"

"Yeah, the service at this place is terrible," Aidan jokes, rising stiffly to his feet. But when he looks over at the kitchen window, he freezes. "No *way*," he says, his jaw hanging open for a second before he bursts out laughing.

"What?" Clare asks, a little sleepily. But even before she

catches sight of them through the window—Scotty and Stella locked in a kiss—she realizes what it must be.

"Are you seeing this?" Aidan asks, shaking his head in disbelief. When he turns and sees her lack of surprise, he stares at her. "You already knew?"

"I just found out."

"Dude," he says with a smile, cuffing her playfully on the shoulder. "You're supposed to tell me these things. How did this happen? How long has it been?"

"Weeks," Clare says. "It's totally nuts. I have no idea how it started. I'll have to get more details at some point."

Aidan shakes his head in wonder. "Scotty and Stella. I did *not* see that coming."

They both turn back to the window, where the two are no longer kissing, but their heads are still close together, and they look happy, happier than Clare can remember seeing either of them in a long time.

"In a weird way," she says, "I think it makes complete sense."

"Yeah?" Aidan asks, clearly still trying to catch up. "Is it just a fling? Or something more?"

"I don't think they know yet."

"Maybe they don't have to," he says, his eyes still trained on the window.

"Yeah, but Stella leaves tomorrow. They're gonna be a *thousand* miles away from each other. How could that ever possibly work?"

"I don't know," Aidan says quietly. "Maybe they'll just see how it goes."

"But that's crazy."

"No crazier than an owl wearing glasses."

"This is much crazier," she says, but in spite of herself, she's smiling.

When they turn back to the window, Scotty and Stella are no longer there. Clare stares at the empty space where they stood only moments ago, and she takes a long breath before looking back over at Aidan.

"Maybe you're right," she says. "Maybe they'll figure something out."

He puts an arm around her shoulders, and the familiar weight of it seems to anchor her right there on the deck, in the very place where he'd once opened a door for her, and where they'd once played footsie. In the place where he'd tripped her, and sneezed on her, and where she'd watched him throw up. In the place where they'd seen an owl that may or may not have been wearing glasses, and where they'd once spent an entire night getting to know each other.

"Maybe this is just the beginning for them," she says, and Aidan smiles.

"Like I said . . . the prologue is the best part."

STOP #12

The Basement

2:33 AM

Outside in Scotty's driveway, they stand in a circle, feeling the full weight of the moment. The time has come to say goodbye, but the words haven't caught up just yet.

A breeze sifts through the branches of the trees that lean close to the house, and a few leaves come twirling down. As she watches them in the glow of the floodlights from the garage, all Clare can think is: *Another ending.*

Right now, together with her best and oldest friends in the deepest part of a late-summer night, she can think of only one thing harder: a new beginning.

"Three months," she says quietly, and nobody has to ask what she means, because they're all thinking the same thing. Already, they're counting the days until Thanksgiving, when they'll all be together again.

"That's not so bad," Stella says, wiggling her toes. She's barefoot, and without her heels, she's actually about the same height as Scotty, who is standing just beside her.

Clare nods. "It's nothing."

"It'll fly."

They look at each other with watery smiles, and then Stella lunges at Clare, throwing her arms around her neck. "It's been...sublime."

Clare smiles. "New word?"

"New day."

"You know," Clare says, her eyes filling as they hug one more time, "Beatrice St. James has nothing on you."

Stella laughs into her shoulder. "That's for sure."

When they pull apart, they see Aidan and Scotty shaking hands, and then, after a pause, thumping each other on the back, before finally working their way up to a hug.

"Don't worry, dude," Scotty says as he steps away. "I'll be sure to look after your sister."

This time, it's Stella who hits him, smacking him squarely across the chest so that his eyes widen in surprise. Aidan only laughs.

"I think you've got your hands pretty full already," he says, nodding at Stella, who gives him a little whack for good measure before diving in for a hug.

"No comments from the peanut gallery," she says into his shoulder, and he laughs again.

"Fair enough. But just know that the peanut gallery is very happy for you."

Scotty skips across the driveway in Clare's direction, a huge grin on his inky face. He doesn't even pause before lifting her off the ground in a giant bear hug.

"Thank you," he says in her ear, and when he sets her down again, she leans back to look at him.

"For what?"

"For thinking I'm good enough."

She gives him a stern look. "How many times do we have to tell you it doesn't matter where you go—"

"No," he says. "For Stella."

"Scotty, come on." She glances over to where Aidan and Stella are waiting near the car. "Of course you're good enough for her. There's no one better."

He grins. "Even though I punched you in the face?"

"So it *was* you?"

"I don't know," he says. "But let's just say it was. It can be my parting gift to Aidan. And you. This way, you don't have to go into freshman year with some crazy story about how your boyfriend gave you a black eye."

"What was that?" Aidan calls out, and Scotty looks over with a laugh.

"I was just telling her that I can't wait to give you another shiner at Thanksgiving."

"You must be joking," Aidan says, puffing out his chest as he strides over. "After a few months of lacrosse practices, you won't stand a chance."

He tucks Scotty under his arm, tousling his mop of hair until it's scrambled as a bird's nest. But this time, they're both laughing, and when Scotty wrenches away, he only pauses for a second before throwing himself back at Aidan for one last hug.

"See you soon, buddy," he says, and Aidan nods.

"I'll call you," Stella tells Clare as she ducks into the car. "Incessantly."

"You'd better," Clare says through the open window as they pull out of the driveway, leaving behind the two pale figures in the dark, each lifting an opposite hand to wave goodbye. The others are clasped between them.

As they wind their way out of Scotty's neighborhood, the headlights cutting across darkened houses and too-bright stop signs, neither of them says anything. In the quiet, Clare swallows a few times, trying her best not to fall apart, because the night isn't over yet, and she knows there are far worse goodbyes still to come.

Beside her, she can tell Aidan is doing the same. After a few minutes, he reaches for the radio, scrolling through channels until he finds something soft and twangy. The glowing clock on the dashboard says it's 2:41 AM, and they're not even bothering to hide the fact that they're yawning now; they just keep passing it back and forth, one and then the other, until they both start to laugh.

"Should we go back to your place?" Aidan asks, and Clare nods hard enough to wake herself up a little.

As they pull into her driveway a few minutes later, they see a shadow pop up in the living room window. Clare unbuckles her seat belt.

"I'm gonna run in before Bingo starts barking," she says, already opening the door. She fishes for her keys as she hurries around to the side of the house. As soon as she's inside, the dog—a floppy-eared, black-and-white tornado of energy—flies at her, thrilled to have some company so long after bedtime.

When Aidan arrives, Bingo goes into overdrive, turning frantic circles at his feet, his tongue lolling out in ecstasy. Clare watches with amusement as Aidan drops to the floor, scratching the dog behind the ears.

In the harsh light of the kitchen, she sees just how terrible his eyes look: two half-moon shadows that will surely turn black and blue before long. His left eye is nearly swollen shut, and below his right eye, the white bandage is now streaked with a thin band of red where the blood is soaking through. She touches a finger lightly to her own temple, conscious of what she must look like as well.

"I think," Aidan says, laughing as the dog licks his ear, "I might miss Bingo the most."

Clare gives him a look of exaggerated outrage, but he's already focused on the dog again, so she wanders over to the kitchen counter, which is tiled with sticky notes covered in her mother's handwriting: reminders for the morning, last-minute to-do lists, notes for Clare. She pulls one off the counter and holds it up for Aidan, who is now lying on his back on the wooden floor of the kitchen, the dog balanced on his stomach.

"Apparently, there's a gift for you on the dining room table," she says, and when he rolls over, Bingo slides right off him into a disgruntled heap.

"For me?" Aidan says, rising to his feet. "That's so nice."

"Don't get too excited," Clare says, crossing into the dining room, where there's a flat, rectangular box on the table. She hands it to Aidan. "I have a feeling it's the same thing they got me."

He rips apart the paper, which is covered in graduation caps—left over from June, but still vaguely appropriate to the occasion—and opens it to reveal a blue towel with his initials embroidered in white across the bottom.

"Wow," he says, running a hand across the soft fabric. His face is tipped down, so his expression is hard to read. "This is...so great."

"You don't have to use it or anything," she says, balling up the wrapping paper. "I told my parents it might be weird to parade around the communal bathrooms with your initials on display. But they thought it'd be handy, you know, for when we have roommates and stuff. And they're obviously big fans of monogramming."

She sweeps an arm around, indicating the vases, picture frames, tote bags, and various other items all emblazoned with her parents' initials. The first time he came over, Aidan had stared at all the floating letters in the room, the giant *R* for *Rafferty* that hangs above the kitchen sink, the printed dishtowels, even the pens on the counter, and when they were finally alone, he couldn't help himself.

"Remind me of your last name again..." he'd said, and her cheeks had blazed with heat. But then he'd hooked a finger into the pocket of her jeans, pulling her forward, and kissed her, right there in the kitchen, with her parents in the next room, and she'd forgotten the question entirely.

Now he folds the towel carefully back into the box. "It's great," he says again, but there's something off about his tone, and Clare realizes a moment too late that his own parents must not have given him anything to mark the occasion.

"I'm sorry," she says, putting a hand on his arm.

"For what?"

Clare shifts from one foot to the other. "Well, your parents..."

"Oh, yeah," he says, brushing this off. "They definitely didn't get me anything. Can you imagine my dad buying something like this? Or buying me anything at all?" He shakes his head. "No, I was just thinking about *your* parents, actually. How good they've been to me."

Clare shrugs. "They're obsessed with you," she says, because it's true. Her parents adore Aidan, who has been around the house constantly over the past couple of years, fixing the cable box, showing them how to save old e-mails, helping her mom slice vegetables before dinner, and taking Bingo for a walk without anyone asking.

"Yeah, but only because *you're* obsessed with me," he says, and before she can even roll her eyes, he corrects himself: "Or were, anyway."

"For the record, I was never obsessed with you," she says. "*You* were obsessed with *me*."

"Okay," he says, holding up his hands. "Let's just agree that nobody was obsessed with anyone. I only meant that your parents think of me as part of the family, but only because I was your boyfriend. And now I'm not." He lifts his shoulders. "It sort of feels like I'm breaking up with them, too."

Clare isn't sure what to say. It's just one more thing she hadn't considered, and as the idea of it settles over her, she realizes again how entwined their lives are. They're like two trees whose branches have grown together. Even if you pull them out by the trunks, they're still going to be twisted and tangled and nearly impossible to separate at the roots.

Just last night at dinner, her dad had asked for the millionth time exactly when Aidan was leaving, and her mom had immediately gotten teary-eyed.

"It's just that it feels like we're losing two members of the family," she said, and Clare had reached out to give her hand a little squeeze.

She can tell they're hoping she and Aidan will stay together, in spite of their own failed attempts to make high school relationships last. But they'd never say it. They're trying to give her enough space to figure this out on her own.

Still, she can almost feel them, eager as a couple of puppies, anxiously waiting to hear whether they'll be able to send Aidan cookies at his new address or wear the UCLA lacrosse shirts he got them or e-mail him when the dishwasher inevitably breaks again.

The dog trots into the dining room with a squeaky toy in

his mouth. It used to be a duck, but the head has long since been chewed off, and there's only one wing still dangling by its side.

"And this guy," Aidan says, bending to give him a pat. "I'm going to miss him like crazy."

"I'm starting to get a complex," Clare says. "I think you might actually like Bingo more than me."

"I like you both," he says. "But you I can always call."

"You can call Bingo, too. My mom leaves him messages on our answering machine all the time. Or you can just wait for Thanksgiving."

Aidan straightens again, fixing her with a solemn look. "So I can still come visit at Thanksgiving?"

"Of *course*," Clare says, about to reach out for him, but then she remembers the state of things, and decides instead on a friendly punch to the shoulder, which is far more awkward than the hug would have been. "My parents would be really sad if you didn't. So would Bingo."

"And you?"

"And me," she says. "Obviously."

He leans against the table, his arms folded. "Yeah, but what if you have a new boyfriend? What if there's some nerdy kid with glasses and loafers who reads Shakespeare in his spare time sitting in my spot?"

"It *would* be nice to have someone who could recite Shakespeare before dinner," she says, tapping her chin thoughtfully, but Aidan is still watching her with a worried expression.

"Seriously," he says, and Clare falls back against the table beside him, so that they're shoulder to shoulder.

"Seriously? I guess it's possible. You could have a new girlfriend by then, too. I don't know if you realize this, but you're kind of a catch."

"Even though you're throwing me back," he says with a half smile. "Like a guppy."

"I'd say you're more of a clown fish," Clare says. "And I'm not throwing you back. I'm setting you free."

Aidan doesn't seem satisfied with this. "But it could happen," he insists. "You and Will Shakespeare. Sitting right here at this table. Eating turkey with your parents. Talking about...I don't know. The plague?"

"I can't think of a single thing I'd rather discuss over dinner," she jokes, but Aidan doesn't smile, and so she shrugs. "Fine. Yeah, I guess it could happen. For you, too. I mean, it's California. Every girl out there is supposed to be blond and tan and ridiculously cool, right? You'll probably meet some model-slash-surfer who plays beach volleyball in her spare time."

Aidan laughs. "Does she skateboard, too?"

"Totally," Clare says. "And she probably designed the skateboard herself."

"She seems talented," he teases. "Sounds like we did pretty well for ourselves."

Clare shakes her head. "See? This is why I really don't want to be thinking about this tonight. Because now I'm getting jealous of some girl who doesn't even exist. Whatever else happens later, tonight is still about us. So I think we should just cross all those other bridges when we come to them."

"Easy breezy," Aidan says with a grin, and Clare nods. "Easy breezy."

He studies her for a few seconds without saying anything, then hitches up one shoulder in a sort of half shrug. "Okay, then," he says finally. "What now?"

They head back into the kitchen to grab a couple of cans of pop from the refrigerator, then slip through the foyer, whispering so they don't wake her parents. At the door to the basement, they make their way downstairs, leaving Bingo—who is afraid of steps—to stand guard at the top.

"I'm gonna miss this place, too," Aidan says as they emerge into the coolness of the basement, and Clare laughs, though she knows he's serious. It's just that it's not much to look at: orange carpeting they've always meant to replace, a maze of pipes across the ceiling, pocked concrete walls, and a random collection of mismatched old furniture.

"It's like the Island of Misfit Toys," her dad had said once, surveying the scene after they'd brought down yet another retired armchair. "This is where good furniture goes to die."

"What movie were *you* watching?" Clare said. "Nobody died on the Island of Misfit Toys."

But she knew what he meant. The basement has always been a kind of way station between the rest of the house and the garbage dump for anything deemed too old. Right now, it holds two mattresses, an ancient couch, an embarrassingly outdated armchair, a scarred coffee table, and a mostly broken TV. The walls are bare except for a single painting of Lake Michigan that her father bought at a garage sale and her mother had already relegated to the basement by the time they made it home.

Aidan walks over to the couch, which is an ugly brown-and-beige plaid, and runs a hand fondly across the back of it. "So," he says with a grin, "any chance we're gonna be revisiting another first while we're here?"

Clare's eyes move from Aidan to the couch, and she feels a wave of nostalgia at the thought of all the nights they've spent curled up there together. It's tempting now to repeat history: to grab his hand and pull him down beside her, to kiss him long enough that the rest of the world disappears, hard enough that she might forget what tomorrow will bring.

But she knows it's more complicated than that—there are rules now, and the fact that they were the ones who set them doesn't matter. The whole thing feels fragile enough without bringing the couch into it.

Besides, she knows exactly what *first* he's talking about, and she can't help flushing at the memory, more recent than some of the others. They'd waited more than a year, until they were both sure, until they were both ready. And then one night last winter, when her parents were out of town, it had happened right here on this couch. Ever since then, they always find themselves smiling in the goofiest possible way whenever they walk down here, as if the couch itself were a shared secret, something too big and too good to remain unnoticed for long.

Now, though, it sits between them like an oversize reminder of all that they're losing.

"We're broken up," she points out, dragging her eyes away from it.

"We could postpone it," he says hopefully. "It seems kind of silly to break up while we're still in the same place, don't you think?"

Clare shakes her head. "It'll just make it worse."

"I highly doubt *that*," he says, walking over to her with a new sense of purpose. He looks at her intently, then starts to lower his head, and for a moment she feels herself falling under the spell of him all over again, this boy with the red hair and bright eyes. Even with all his cuts and bruises, she's struck by how familiar the terrain of his face is, all the many freckles and lines, and she wonders if she'll ever know another person by heart like this. But just before his lips touch hers, she snaps back, remembering all over again, and leans away.

"Aidan," she says in a low voice, and he stands very still for a few beats, his mouth parted. Then he shakes his head and straightens up again.

"Yeah," he says. "You're right."

They blink at each other, neither of them moving.

"It's just that—"

"I know," he says. "You don't have to explain. We broke up. This is part of it. I guess I just didn't want it to be. At least for a little while."

"I know," she says, looking away. She takes a few steps backward, bumping into the Ping-Pong table, which is the only thing actually purchased specifically for this room. She reaches behind her for one of the worn paddles, relieved to have stumbled across a distraction, and holds it up.

"Should we try one last time?"

"Sure," he says, walking over to the other side of the table. "But this isn't going to be half as much fun as what I had in mind."

"It will if we break our record."

"It's been forever since we've even come close," he says, picking up the paddle and giving it a twirl. "But I'm game if you are."

"Oh, I'm game," she says, serving the ball to him. He lobs it back in her direction, and then she does the same, again and again until the orange ball is nothing but a blur. There are plenty of opportunities for them to wing it hard at each other, but instead, they do their best to continue the rally, both of them counting silently as the ball flies back and forth, back and forth, until Aidan finally sends it spinning into the net.

"Sixty-two," Clare announces. "Not even close."

"Pitiful," he agrees. "We can do better."

They volley for a while longer, and this time the long

chain is broken when Clare accidentally slices a shot hard to the left, the ball hitting the very edge of the table before it sails past Aidan and rolls under the couch.

"Jeez," he says as he flattens himself on the carpet, reaching for the ball. "You're kind of intimidating with that shiner."

Clare spins her paddle a few times and makes a menacing face. "Oh, yeah?"

"Yeah," he says, returning with the dusty ball. "Quite the bruiser."

"You too," she says. "Double bruiser."

They begin again, and this time they make it to ninety-eight before Clare misses.

"Not bad," she says as she retrieves the ball. "Have you been practicing without me?"

"No," he says stiffly.

She frowns at him. "I'm only kidding. It's fine if you were."

Aidan has a Ping-Pong table in his own basement, but the only time Clare was ever down there, she noticed that it was completely covered with piles of laundry and oversize boxes of paper towels.

"We haven't used ours since I was little," he says, swinging the paddle absently. "I tried to get Riley to play a couple months ago, but it's not really her thing."

"Do you ever..."

"What?"

"Never mind."

"No," he says. "Do I ever what?"

"Play with your dad?"

He snorts. "Seriously?"

"Seriously."

"Of course not," he says, rubbing at an invisible spot on the table with this thumb. "That would be considered fun. And my dad doesn't do fun. My dad only does what he wants to do...." His voice breaks, and he lifts his eyes to meet Clare's. "I bet he won't even see me off tomorrow."

"Of course he will," she says, troubled at the thought. "They're driving you to the airport, right? That's all part of the whole college deal. The dramatic goodbye, the bear hugs, looking back to see them waiting while you get in line at security..."

"I think you're describing a different movie than mine," he says with a pained smile. "At this point, I'll be lucky if he even says goodbye before my mom and I head out."

"You had a fight. That's all. He'll be over it by tomorrow," she says, trying to sound more certain than she feels, then adds, "It's too big a deal not to be."

"Maybe," Aidan says, but he doesn't sound convinced. He juts his chin in Clare's direction, and she realizes she's still clutching the tiny orange ball. "Let's play."

It takes a while for them to get a good rhythm going again; each time they get past twenty or so, one of them whiffs.

"We can always stop, you know," Clare says, but Aidan's face is set with determination, and instead of answering, he just widens his stance and holds up his paddle, so she serves it to him yet again.

Over and over, they try and fail. The ball glances off the corner of the table, or Clare misjudges the distance and misses entirely, or Aidan spikes it into the net with more force than seems strictly necessary.

They're both tired. Clare's limbs feel heavy, and she can see that Aidan is fighting back yawns between rallies. With each new attempt, they seem to fall apart quicker. But every time she moves to end the game, Aidan just frowns and motions for her to continue.

"We can do this," he says. "We've done it before."

"That was a million years ago," she points out. Soon after they started dating, they'd wandered down here and picked up the paddles, half-jokingly. But after a few practice swings, they realized they were both pretty good, and they managed to keep it going for 188 consecutive volleys, whooping and cheering after the ball finally sailed away. Right now, though, that feels like a very long time ago. "We're nowhere close. We might set the record for number of attempts at the record, but that's about it."

Aidan only shakes his head. "Let's go," he says, so they try again.

After a while, in the middle of a rally, Clare feels a wave of exhaustion wash over her, and without thinking about it, she simply snatches the ball out of the air when it comes spinning in her direction.

"I can't," she says, when she sees Aidan's crestfallen expression. "I'm too tired."

"But we were so close," he says, though they both know that's not true. "We can do it. We have to."

Clare leans forward on the table and fixes him with an even look. "I'm going to tell you the same thing you told me earlier," she says. "This is not a metaphor."

His face doesn't change, so she tries again.

"It doesn't mean anything. It's just a stupid challenge."

"Yeah, but"—he tosses his paddle onto the table in frustration—"if we beat the record..."

"What?" she asks impatiently.

He lowers his eyes. "Then the whole night won't just be about us breaking up."

"Aidan," she says, softening a bit. "It won't be. Look how much we've done tonight. If anything, it'll be the night we picked Scotty up from jail. Or the night he gave himself about a thousand tattoos."

Aidan smiles, but there's something somber about it. "The rest of it doesn't matter," he says. "Trust me. When we look back on tonight, all we're gonna remember is that we broke up."

"And you think Ping-Pong will help?"

"Maybe," he says, and he looks so earnest right now, so sincere, that it's all she can do to stay on her side of the table. "It could have been the night we set the Ping-Pong record instead."

She laughs. "You're crazy if you think that would outrank our breakup. You think I'd look back one day and remember this"—she holds up the ball—"instead of losing you?"

He moves around the table, taking a few slow steps in her direction. "It was worth a try," he says, closing the space between them. When they're only a few inches apart, she tips her head back to look at him. "And you're not losing me. I'm losing you."

"Either way," she manages to say around the knot that's formed in her throat.

He reaches out and tucks a loose strand of hair behind her ear, then lets his hand linger on her neck, and the feel of his skin on hers sends a shot of electricity through her. She can see the couch out of the corner of her eye, and her face prickles with a sudden warmth.

This is the thing about Aidan. This has always been the thing about him. He makes her forget all her reasons and rules and plans.

He makes her forget about everything but him.

"It'd have to be something a lot bigger," she says, and he widens his eyes in exaggerated astonishment.

"Bigger than hitting a Ping-Pong ball a hundred and eighty-nine times in a row?"

She nods.

"What could be bigger than that?" he says, but even as he does, Clare sees it happen: his gaze falling on the only painting to brighten the concrete walls, a sweeping watercolor of Lake Michigan in the winter, icy and hardened and dusted with snow. When his eyes flick back to her, she's already shaking her head.

"No."

He grins. "Yes."

"No way," she says more firmly, but it doesn't matter: He's already pacing back and forth in excitement.

"It's perfect," he says, turning away. "No, it's *epic*. Nobody's ever done it. And there's no way it wouldn't be memorable." He pauses in front of the couch, turning to her with a triumphant look. "It's just big enough."

"It's too big," she says flatly. "And too stupid."

"Sorry," he says, clapping his hands. "It's a done deal. This is happening."

"You seriously want to jump into Lake Michigan right now? Think about how cold it will be. And aren't you tired?"

"Nope," he says with a laugh. "I'm wide awake."

Clare's eyes wander over to the couch again, and then back to Aidan. He's all lit up by his idea, smiling so hard that the bandage beneath his eye is losing its grip. Something about the sight of him—so eager to make the best of this night—makes her heart swell, and she sets down her Ping-Pong paddle.

"Well," she says. "Don't I at least get to suggest something, too?"

He gives her a skeptical look. "There's no way you have a better idea."

"Maybe I do."

"Better than saving Rusty?" he asks, clearly tickled at the prospect. "Not possible."

"You don't even want to hear it?"

He shakes his head. "Nope," he says. "There's literally nothing in the world that I want to do more than save that stupid robot right now."

"Okay," Clare says, walking over to the couch, next to where Aidan has stopped his pacing just beside the coffee table. "I'm in."

"Great," he says with an officious nod. "Then we should probably get going."

But just before he can walk away, she reaches out and grabs his hand. He spins around again, the smile slipping from his face, replaced by a look of confusion.

"I'm in," she repeats, feeling uncharacteristically bold. "But I still think we should try mine first."

It takes a moment for this to register—the way she's looking at him, the way her hand is clasped in his—and when it does, his expression changes to one of surprise.

"Oh," he says, his mouth caught in the shape of the word. His eyebrows shoot up high on his forehead, loosening the bandage further. *"Oh."*

"Yeah," she says, tugging him a little closer. "What do you think?"

A few seconds pass as they study each other, and then his face cracks open again, his smile broadening, and he dives onto the couch without letting go of her hand, pulling her down with him, so that they end up tangled there together.

"I think," he says, as they rearrange themselves, his face very close to hers, his breath warm and sweet, "that it sounds like a *very* good plan."

She reaches up and runs her fingers over the bandage beneath his right eye, pressing it gently back into place. "Good."

"Though still not as good as mine."

"Shut up," she says, but even as she does, his lips are meeting hers, and they're both fighting back smiles, because for once, he already has.

STOP #13

The Lake

3:54 AM

The inner tube that's tucked under Clare's arm begins to flap in the breeze the moment they hit the sand.

"This," she says, holding it tighter, "is a terrible idea."

But Aidan isn't listening. He's already plunging ahead toward the water, which is almost indistinguishable from the beach in the darkness. Only the sound of the waves and the wedge of moonlight across the surface give it away.

Clare has never been out here so late before—or so early, really, given that it's nearly four AM now—and as she stumbles toward the shoreline, she wonders if it's always so windy at this time of night. Together, they trudge ahead beneath the waning moon, their feet sinking deep into the cool sand with each step.

Back in the basement, this whole endeavor had sounded vaguely unappealing, but still with some potential to be good fun. Now, though, with the rush of waves loud in her ears, the night deep and vast all around her, it seems downright insane.

"This is a really stupid idea," she says again, but Aidan's head is lost in his shirt, which he's trying to peel off. When he finds his way out of it, he tosses it to the ground beside him, and looks over as if he'd forgotten she was there.

"What?" he asks, unbuttoning his jeans and then stepping out of them. He stands there watching her, wearing only his blue boxers, looking pale in the moonlight. But his face is set and determined, and already he's swinging his arms in circles to loosen up.

"I don't think you should do this."

"It's fine," he says, hopping from one foot to the other. "It's just a little late-night swim." He stops and grins at her. "You could come, too."

"No way," she says, shuddering a little. "It's too dark. And the water's freezing. And I'm sure it's a lot farther out than it looks."

"That's the whole point."

"What is?"

"It can't be epic if there's no challenge to it," he says simply, and then reaches out for the inner tube. She hands it over reluctantly. It's hard to tell if the thing will even float. She found it in the back of the hall closet, left over from a few years ago, when her dad broke his tailbone trying to prove he could still play hockey on his fiftieth birthday. For weeks, he couldn't sit down without the black inflatable doughnut.

Now, if Aidan succeeds, Rusty will wear it proudly on

his skinny metal neck: a lifeline for the perpetually drowning robot.

Aidan turns it over in his hands a few times with a smile. "Sometimes the hardest things are the ones most worth doing."

"Who said *that*?"

He shrugs. "Me."

"Come on."

"Fine. My dad."

Clare frowns at him. "Is that what this is about? Because you know you don't have to prove anything...."

"I know," he says, looking back at the water impatiently. Above them, the clouds have parted and the stars are crowded and bright. Clare shivers as a sharp wind cuts right through her thin sweater.

"I don't think you do," she says. "Look, you made your choice, and it's a good one. Now you have to let yourself off the hook. Your dad will get over it at some point."

"What if he doesn't?"

"He will," she says firmly. "But even if not..."

Aidan folds his arms across his chest. "Even if not, this is still something I need to do for myself."

"But why?" she asks. "This is crazy."

"It's our last night. Everything's ending. I can't think of a better time to do something crazy." He tilts his head at her. "Can you?"

"I guess not," she says eventually, though she's still uneasy. "But if you drown out there, I'm going to kill you."

He laughs. "Fair enough."

"Just be careful," she says more seriously, and he gives her a little salute.

"I will."

"And hurry up, okay? Rusty's been waiting a really, really long time."

As he goes loping off toward the water, Clare realizes this might be the happiest she's seen him all night. Just before wading in, he turns back to wave. Even in the dark, she can see that he's grinning wildly.

"It's freezing," he yells, the words hollowed out by the wind.

Clare takes a few steps in the direction of the shore, watching as—all at once—he turns and plows into the water, running hard against the waves until it's deep enough for him to dive in and start swimming.

As soon as he disappears, she feels a sudden, choking panic. For a few minutes, there's the blur of his white arms in the moonlight, but it's not long before she can't even see that. She walks up to the edge of the surf, straining her eyes against the darkness, which is so thick it feels like some sort of curtain has been pulled across the line between the land and the water, with only the moon left to peek through.

Glancing at her watch, she wishes she'd noted the time when he took off, or that she'd thought to start counting, to somehow mark the minutes as they pass. She pulls out her cell phone and switches on the flashlight feature, trying to see farther into the darkness, but the dim light is swallowed whole before it makes it even a few feet.

She knows that Aidan's right: It's only a swim. But the night is black and the wind is cold and the beach feels like the loneliest place on earth right now. She keeps her eyes trained on the bobbing robot in the distance, which is topped by a small winking light, like a star that fell out of the sky. From here, it might as well be a million miles away, and Clare finds herself thinking about what Aidan said: *It can't be epic if there's no challenge to it.*

Standing alone on the shore, she's aware of how few challenges she's ever faced. All her life, everything has come easily to her. She's always been at the head of her class, always excelled at tests and scored well on essays, always been a favorite of most of her teachers. And if you look at it just the right way, that might seem impressive. But Clare knows the truth: None of it was very difficult.

And now here she is, going off to college completely untested. Even if she hadn't sailed through so much in life, her parents still would have been proud of her, and she's grateful for that. But she realizes that she's never had any-one to push her—truly push her—except Aidan, who was willing to jump into a freezing-cold lake in the middle of the night just to prove something to himself, while Clare stayed behind, warm and dry and completely alone.

It occurs to her for the first time that maybe this is why she decided to break up with him. Not because it was the right thing to do, but because it seemed like the *easy* thing.

Staying together, on the other hand, would be hard.

It would be the hardest thing imaginable: trying to make it work while being apart. Because what if it turns out her heart isn't built for that kind of distance? What if it's like a radio: clear and bright up close, but blurry and full of static from far away?

She blinks into the darkness, imagining Aidan alone out there in the freezing water.

Sometimes the hardest things are the ones most worth doing.

She knows for sure now that must be true.

But still, there's no sign of him. She scans the horizon for what feels like the thousandth time, trying to swallow her fear. He's out there all alone, and there's no way to know if he needs her, no way to tell if he's okay.

This is how it will be from now on: Aidan, far away and drifting farther.

She hears a distant rumble of thunder, and out across the water, a crack of lightning flashes bright across the rough surface. With it, the panic she's been trying to push away comes clawing back, jagged and desperate, and she realizes her hands are shaking. She lifts her phone, fumbling with it for a second before typing in the only three numbers flashing through her head right now—9-1-1—so that they'll be that much closer if she should need them. When she's done, she lowers the phone again and squints out at the water, her eyes stinging from the wind and her heart pounding so hard it hurts.

"Come on, Aidan," she says under her breath.

But there's nothing: just a sweep of water as flat and black as a chalkboard, and another far-off growl of thunder. She thinks once more about Aidan's words, which are still jangling around in her head, and then she makes a decision.

Before she can begin to overthink it, she kicks off her sandals and takes a step forward. When the first wave rushes over her feet, she stiffens, stunned by the icy temperature, newly frightened at the thought of Aidan having already been out there so long. But she knows if she's going to do this, she has to keep moving, so she plunges ahead, her teeth chattering as the water rises to her calves and then her knees and then finally the bottom of her dress, which drags behind her as she pushes forward.

Just before diving in, she takes a big gulp of air, trying to prepare herself. But still, the cold comes as a shock: frigid and bracing and more powerful than she could have imagined. Her numb legs instantly begin churning of their own accord, and her hands move through the water by instinct. As she starts to swim, her body begins to adjust: the goose bumps subsiding, her limbs growing looser as she propels herself through the water, unable to see where she's going.

But she doesn't notice any of that.

All she cares about is reaching Aidan.

She's not sure how long she's been swimming, night-blind and cold and disoriented, when she pauses to lift her head, gasping for breath. She finds the blinking light of the buoy and scans the water for Aidan, and when she spots

201

him there in the distance—a flash of white, inching slowly toward the shore—she goes weak with relief. She throws her head back and lets out a laugh, the sound of it bright and tinny in the dark.

"Aidan," she yells, and he lifts his head as he catches sight of her. He calls out something in return, but the words are lost to the wind, and then he's swimming toward her once more, paddling doggedly in her direction, and with a shiver, she starts moving again, too.

They're not far apart now, maybe half the length of a football field, and in the light of the moon, she can see him stop every few strokes to wave at her, bobbing up and down like some sort of damaged buoy.

This time, when he calls out her name, she can finally hear him.

"Hi," she yells back, and he spins around to point at something behind him.

"Did you see?"

"I can't see anything!"

"I did it," he says breathlessly, splashing over to her. "I actually did it."

When he's near enough, Clare reaches out and loops her arms around him, and she can feel his muscles go limp. But he holds on to her waist, and they stay there like that for a long time, both of them too winded to talk as they cling to each other, their legs still moving frantically beneath the surface.

"I love you," she says softly, and he leans back to look at

her. There's a drop of water hanging from his nose, and his lips look bluish, even in the dark.

"What was that?" he asks with a grin. "I think I might have some water in my ear. Did you say you dove me?"

She shakes her head, gripping him a little harder. "I *love* you," she says again, and as she does, a wave catches them, sending them floating up for a second before dipping them back down again, and it feels like a roller coaster, like a bump in the road, the kind that sends your heart up into your throat, the kind that sets you flying.

Aidan kisses her then, and it's cold and wet and shivery, but there's also a heat to it that warms her from the inside out. "I love you, too."

She can feel him shaking all over now, and she realizes she's doing the same.

"We should get you back," she tells him, but he only tightens his hold on her.

"Not yet," he says quietly. "Just a few more seconds."

Clare doesn't argue.

She's not ready to let go yet, either.

STOP #14

The Gallaghers' House (Again)

4:48 AM

Even as they tiptoe up the stairs to Aidan's bedroom, he's busy reliving the events of the night.

"It was like one of those ring-toss games at a carnival," he whispers, his face still all lit up. He stops to demonstrate—with a flick of his wrist—the way he'd managed to throw the inner tube over the top of Rusty's skinny frame after only three tries, as Clare gives him a little nudge to keep him moving forward.

This is possibly the worst place in the world to be recounting the tale: standing on the Gallaghers' front staircase with his parents asleep just yards away. Their clothes are dripping on the ugly gray carpet of the steps, and Clare's teeth are still chattering; in the water, the moment the adrenaline had faded into relief, she'd started to shiver and hadn't stopped since. Everything about her—from her nose to her toes—feels brittle and numb, so when Aidan turns around, she prods him forward again.

"Sweatshirt," she reminds him.

"Right, sorry," he says, walking up a few more steps before stopping once more. "It *was* pretty cool, though, right?"

Clare nods. "Very, very cool."

In his room, Aidan digs through a pile of clothes at the foot of his bed.

"Harvard or UCLA?" he asks, holding up two oversize hoodies.

"The big question," she says, then reaches for the blue one with UCLA printed in huge letters across the front.

Aidan smiles. "Good choice."

"I agree," Clare says, peeling off her wet dress and practically diving into the fleecy sweatshirt, which comes down nearly to her knees. "Got anything else for me?"

He tosses her a pair of gray sweatpants. And then, for good measure, some woolen mittens, too.

"I know you're joking," she says, tugging them on, "but I'm totally wearing them."

When they've both changed, Aidan studies her with amusement. She's swimming in his sweatshirt, and though she's rolled up the sweatpants several times, they still drag at the bottom. She claps her mittened hands together with a quiet *thump*.

"Perfect," she says. "Now what?"

He considers this for a moment. "Hot chocolate, I think."

"Brilliant," she says, and as he walks over to the door, he grabs the hood of her sweatshirt and rucks it up over her head.

"*Now* it's perfect," he says with a grin.

Downstairs, they pull the canister of cocoa and a couple of mugs from the cupboard, then heat up the milk. They do their best to be quiet, skidding around in their socks, being sure to close each cabinet with exaggerated care. When the hot chocolate is ready, they sit at the kitchen table with their hands cupped around mugs, reveling in the warmth before taking a sip.

"I can't believe we did that," Aidan says after a little while.

"You did it," Clare points out.

"Well, sure," he says, puffing up with pride again. "I mean, if we're being really technical about it, I guess I *did* save the unofficial town mascot, who *has* been flailing out there for years without anyone else to rescue him."

Clare hides her smile with her mug. "So modest."

"But you came after me," he says, leaning forward on the table. "You forgot all about the rules for a minute. You didn't think for a second about what an idiotic thing it is to do, jumping into the lake in the middle of the night. You just did it."

"Yeah, but—"

"Yeah, but nothing," he says, banging his palm against the table in his enthusiasm, which sets their cups rattling. "This is why you need to stop worrying so much about everything. Don't get me wrong, I love the way your mind works, but when you shut it off for a minute, look what happens."

"I do really idiotic things?"

"That's not what I mean," he says. "The way you've been so worried about your major, and what you want to do with your life, and all that—"

"Right," she says. "All those tiny little details."

"—that's the version of you that sits back on the shore. But really, you should just be diving right in, you know?"

Clare ducks her head. "Maybe."

"That's what college is for—you're supposed to try new things even if it means making mistakes. If you stop over-thinking everything, maybe you'll have a little more fun." He sits back again, looking pleased with himself. "That's always been my philosophy, anyway."

She laughs. "You might be on to something."

"Of course I am," he says. "I'm kind of a genius when it comes to giving advice."

"And saving robots."

"That, too," he says, smiling at her from across the table. He holds her gaze for a long time, long enough to make her wonder whether he's thinking the same thing she is: that what happened back there in the water—what happened back in her basement, even—might have been enough to shift things between them yet again. That maybe the pen-dulum has swung back in the other direction. That maybe they still have a chance.

That maybe it's even something she wants.

Almost as if he can read her thoughts, Aidan lifts his mug. "To you and me," he says, and they clink glasses, the hot chocolate sloshing over the sides. Clare is about to use

208

the sleeve of the sweatshirt to mop up the spill when Aidan holds up a hand to stop her. He points at the logo on his own hoodie.

"Please," he says, pulling his hand into the cuff at a purely theatrical pace, then rubbing at the spot on the table.

"Such a gentleman," Clare says, sitting back again.

"Not at all," Aidan says cheerfully. "I just wanted to make sure we use the right one as a rag."

They're both startled by a voice behind them.

"Very mature," Mr. Gallagher says, his face twisted into a frown. He's leaning against the doorframe, a nubby blue bathrobe tied over his plaid pajamas, and without his glasses, his eyes look fuzzy and unfocused. His hair, which is usually neatly combed, is sticking up at the back, so that he almost looks like a little boy just waking up from a nap.

Clare glances back at Aidan, waiting for him to say something, but it's clear right away that that's not going to happen. His eyes are on the table, his arms folded tightly across the Harvard logo on his shirt, his jaw stubbornly jutted.

"I hope we didn't wake you," Clare says, but Mr. Gallagher doesn't seem to hear her: He's too busy staring at Aidan, his face gone slack with surprise.

"What happened to you?"

"Nothing," Aidan says, lowering his chin as he tries his best to hide his swollen eyes.

"'Nothing' must have a pretty good right hook," Mr.

Gallagher says, but then his gaze lands on Clare, and he looks even more alarmed. "You two weren't—"

"No," Clare says quickly. "We're fine. There was just a misunderstanding at a party, and we got a little bit mixed up in it, but everything's okay. Really."

He stares at her for a few more beats, trying to decide whether to believe her. She doesn't blame him for being horrified to find them in the kitchen at five in the morning with a pair of matching shiners, and she wouldn't blame him if he sent Aidan to his room and then marched her home right this minute. But a few more seconds pass in slightly startled silence, and then his shoulders relax, and he sighs, apparently having decided to give them the benefit of the doubt. "Do you need some ice or something?"

"We iced them a bunch before," she says, smiling brightly. "Really, it's fine. Looks worse than it is." She touches a finger to her eye. "I keep forgetting about it, actually."

He glances back to Aidan one more time, still trying to absorb all this, and then, finally, walks over to the stove and grabs the teakettle. While he fills it at the sink, Clare shoots Aidan a look. She can see that his mind is whirring as he tries to come up with an escape plan.

But once the kettle is on, Mr. Gallagher pulls out a chair, and there's a long, uncomfortable silence. Clare smiles politely while Aidan sits there fidgeting with the fraying drawstrings of his hoodie.

"Must've been some party," Mr. Gallagher says. "You two are out pretty late."

There's no accusation in his voice; in fact, he looks just as awkward as his son right now, and Clare can tell how hard he's trying.

"Last night in town," she says with a forced cheerfulness. "There was a lot to do. And a few last goodbyes."

"Are you excited about Dartmouth?"

"I am," she says, bobbing her head a little too hard.

"Do you know what you'll be studying yet?"

"I have no idea, actually," she says, glancing in Aidan's direction with a little smile. Maybe it was his speech, or just the shock of the freezing-cold water, but somehow, she no longer feels quite so daunted by all that's ahead. She might never be like Aidan: carefree and spontaneous and largely untroubled. But in her own way, she feels ready to dive in. And that's enough for now.

"I'm still figuring that out," she tells Mr. Gallagher, and this time she kind of likes the sound of it.

"Well, you've got time," he says, his eyes shifting back to Aidan, who's staring at his hot chocolate as if it might turn out to be a portal to some other room, some other place entirely. "If you're at an Ivy, it almost doesn't matter what you major in—you'll have a lot of opportunities, no matter what."

Clare lowers her eyes, tucking a strand of damp hair behind her ear. "Hey, did you know that UCLA has this really cool summer program in sports management—"

"Clare," Aidan says in a low voice. "Don't."

"All I'm saying is that there are a lot of opportunities at UCLA, too—"

This time, Aidan sets his mug down hard on the table. *"Clare."*

Nobody says anything for a moment, and then Mr. Gallagher leans back in his chair, the back legs creaking. "I'm sure that's true," he says, just as the kettle begins to whistle on the stove, and he hurries over before it can wake anyone else.

As he pours himself a cup of tea, Clare has an idea. "You know," she says, avoiding Aidan's eyes, "I just realized what time it is. I should probably call my parents and let them know I'll be home pretty soon."

Aidan gives her a withering look, but Clare is already pushing her chair back from the table, pointing helplessly at her phone, as if she has no choice in the matter.

She doesn't go far, though. Just outside the kitchen, she hovers in the doorway, listening as Mr. Gallagher sits back down at the table. She waits there, because she wants to hear him apologize. She wants to hear him say he's looking forward to driving Aidan to the airport in the morning. She wants to hear him admit how much he'll miss his son.

But instead, they sit in silence for a full minute before he says, "So you must be sad to say goodbye to Clare."

Aidan's tone is curt. "Obviously."

"You know, your mother and I were long-distance for a little while when I was in the navy."

"I know."

"It wasn't easy," Mr. Gallagher says, his voice sounding somehow faraway. "In fact, it was one of the hardest things

212

I've ever done. But it was worth it. Usually the hardest things are the ones most—"

"I know, Dad."

"Do you?"

Aidan heaves a mighty sigh. "I know you think I don't know the meaning of hard work, but you're wrong. The problem isn't that I don't try. It's that we don't always agree on what's worth it. For me, Harvard wasn't. So I didn't try. Simple as that."

"I wasn't talking about Harvard," Mr. Gallagher says, clearing his throat. "I was talking about you and Clare."

"So, what?" Aidan says, a challenge in his voice. "You don't think I can do that, either?"

His father's tone is patient. "I didn't say that. You two actually seem great together. I happen to think she brings out the best in you."

Aidan has no comeback for this, and from the next room, Clare can't help smiling. There's a short silence between them, and then, quietly, he says, "That's true."

"So," Mr. Gallagher says, "what's your plan, then? Are you two staying together?"

The answer comes swiftly, and it has a kind of force to it, a momentum that—even from the next room—is nearly enough to flatten her.

"No," Aidan says, the word vibrating in the stillness of the house.

No pause, no hesitation, no waffling.

That's it. Just: *no*.

Clare feels herself go numb as she tries to absorb this, the conversation in the next room oddly muffled by the static in her head. Already, they've moved on to something else—she hears Aidan say something about his flight tomorrow—and their voices are softer now, less accusatory, which is exactly what she'd hoped for.

Only she can't listen anymore.

Instead, she crosses the darkened dining room and escapes into the foyer, where she sits down at the bottom of the stairs they'd climbed together only a short while ago, hugging her knees to her chest.

It's her fault. It makes no sense for her to be caught off guard by this. They'd decided—*she'd* decided—to break up, and whatever else might have happened since then was clearly all in her head. The couch, the lake, all those big moments—none of it mattered, because of one simple fact: They'd never decided to *un*-break up.

She feels her eyes prick with tears, more out of humiliation than anything else. How can she have been stupid enough to let her guard down now? After she'd done such a good job convincing Aidan they should be apart, good enough to make him spit the word like a bullet: *no*.

She takes a deep breath, willing herself not to cry. Maybe it was hearing it said out loud for the first time, or maybe it's just that she's tired, and sad, and the night behind her feels like a hundred nights all rolled into one. But whatever it is, she lets it sweep over her now, hunched on the staircase as the clock in the hallway chimes in low, rounded tones.

She's not sure how long she's been sitting there when she hears footsteps. She lifts her head to glance toward the dining room first, but then realizes they're coming from above, and she twists to see Riley at the top of the stairs.

Her hair is mussed and tangled, and she's wearing a pair of blue-checked pajama pants with an old Chicago Bears T-shirt. Clare opens her mouth to say something, but Riley puts a finger to her lips as she makes her way from one step to the next, expertly avoiding the creaky spots.

"Hi," she says when she gets to the bottom, dropping down beside Clare. She rubs at her eyes and yawns. "What's going on?"

"They're talking," Clare says, and she can feel her lip quiver as she does. She takes another long breath to steady herself. "Aidan and your dad."

It's only now that Riley seems to register that she's upset. She tilts her head, looking at Clare with concern. "That's a good thing," she says with an encouraging smile, and Clare wipes at her nose with the back of her hand.

"I know," she says, and then all at once, she can't help it anymore: She feels her face start to crumple, and the tears arrive in a rush. "I'm really happy," she manages to say, the words coming out in a sob, wet and muddled.

For a moment, Riley just stares at her, and Clare blinks back, neither of them quite sure what to say. And then, just like that, they both burst into laughter. Clare cups a hand over her mouth, realizing how loud they're being, but Riley doesn't even bother. She's still waking up, and the whole thing—finding her brother's girlfriend crying on the stairs in the early hours of the morning—is too much for her.

"Well, you definitely *look* really happy," she says, still laughing, and then—when Clare's smile begins to slip again without warning—Riley slings an arm around her shoulders and gives her a little squeeze.

"Yeah, I know," she says, letting her head rest against Clare's. "I'm gonna miss him, too."

STOP # 15

The Car

5:42 AM

In the driveway, everything feels eerily similar to the way the night started: the blank stare of the garage door through the windshield, Aidan beside her with a hand on the keys, the car filled with uncertainty and nervous anticipation.

If this were a board game, they'd have made a full circle by now, finally reaching the end, though from where Clare is sitting, it's hard to tell whether they've lost or won.

"So he's driving me to the airport," Aidan says, letting his hand slide off the keys as he looks over at her. His voice is filled with such undisguised relief that it's almost enough to push the earlier *no* out of her head.

"That's great," she says, clasping her hands in her lap so that she doesn't accidentally reach out for one of his. "I'm so glad."

"I mean, I don't think he'll be waving a UCLA flag anytime soon, but I guess he's trying," he says. "He said he was sorry for putting so much pressure on me that I felt like I had to lie. And then I said I was sorry for actually lying. And then he said he was sorry for how he reacted to my lie. And then I said I was sorry for how I reacted to how *he* reacted to my lie. It was kind of like a game of dominoes, only with apologies."

"That's great," Clare begins, but Aidan rushes on, clearly unable to contain his excitement.

"He even said he'd think about coming out for Parents' Weekend, which probably just means he'll go golfing while Mom goes to all the events with me, but I'll take it," he says, laughing. "I mean, it's crazy, right? A few months ago—even just *yesterday*—I never would've imagined any of this would be..." He trails off, looking over at her with shiny eyes. "Thank you. Really."

"For what?"

"For being so spectacularly unsubtle about forcing us to talk," he says. "And for mentioning the sports-management thing. Turns out, he was really interested in that."

"Something you have in common," she says. "Imagine that."

Aidan smiles in spite of himself. "So what now?"

Clare isn't sure how to answer that. Part of her just wants to go home and collapse onto her bed amid all the boxes and suitcases until they have to leave. She's having a hard time shaking the heaviness that has settled over her, and if they're going to have to say goodbye soon anyway— if this is indeed the end—then maybe they should just put themselves out of their misery now.

But she can feel Aidan's eyes on her, and something

about his gaze stops her from saying so. "Well," she says, "we're almost out of time, and we're definitely out of stops, so..."

"Good," Aidan says, turning the key in the ignition. "Because I thought of one more."

She doesn't ask where they're going. Instead, she rests her head against the cool of the window and tries not to let the motion of the car put her to sleep. Aidan drives slowly, drumming his fingers on the steering wheel to some unknowable tune. Ahead of them, the grayish sky is streaked with pink now, the bright ball of sun just starting to burn through the trees as they head east toward the water.

"We're not going down to the lake again, are we?" she asks, and Aidan gives her a cryptic look.

"You'll see."

But when they reach the entrance to the beach, he turns left instead, and they weave through the quiet neighborhood that sits along the edge of the water. The houses are still mostly dark but for the occasional light in an upstairs window, and Clare realizes that the people inside are preparing themselves to start a brand-new day, while she and Aidan are still finishing out the last one, which somehow manages to feel like both the world's longest and shortest day all at the same time.

Clare sits up and tucks her hands into the pocket of her hoodie. "I sort of thought you might be going back to check on Rusty."

"Nah, he's fine. In fact, I'm sure he's downright buoyant this morning."

She rolls her eyes. "We forgot to get a souvenir."

"There wasn't much to grab except bolts and screws," Aidan says, braking to let a squirrel pass on the empty road ahead of them. "And I think that might have been getting into felony territory."

"I guess it doesn't matter, anyway. We forgot a bunch of other places, too."

He nods. "The fountain. And Scotty's house."

"And yours. And jail..."

"Oh, I got some pictures of Scotty. I can't imagine a better souvenir than that. We should have swiped something from Andy Kimball's house, though. And the bowling alley."

"Next time I'm there, I'll be sure to steal a napkin or something."

"A napkin? Who steals a napkin from a bowling alley? Where's the challenge in that?"

"It was never supposed to be a challenge," she tells him. "Just a memento."

"Yeah, but if you're gonna do it, you've gotta do it right," he says as he comes to a stop at an intersection. "Smuggling a bowling ball out of there would've been amazing."

"I'm not sure it would make much sense to lug a bowling ball all the way to New Hampshire. But I take your point."

"Sometimes the hardest things—"

"—are the ones most worth doing," she finishes, and he looks over at her with a smile, then flicks the button for the radio, which is still tuned to the same bluegrass station from earlier. A song—slow and warbling—fills the car, and Clare lowers her window to let her arm dangle outside, feeling the heat of the still-rising sun, and the wind rushing in, warm and sweet and new.

When she realizes they're just a few blocks away from the high school, she glances over at Aidan, the question left unspoken, but he shakes his head anyway.

"Nope."

In town, they pass the fountain in the village square, where a few birds are taking a morning bath, then Slices, which is shuttered and empty at this time of day. It feels like they're reliving the night all over again, and she wonders if that's the point of this, or whether the town is just so small that they can't help passing everything more than once on any given drive.

When they catch a light at the corner near the gas station, Clare remembers the stash of candy still in the back of the car. She grabs a roll of Smarties and offers one to Aidan, who is already holding out a flattened palm.

Finally, as they loop back toward the other end of the main street, she gives up.

"We're going in circles," she informs him, and Aidan nods.

"Yep."

"Why?"

"Why not?"

"I don't get it."

221

"This is it," he says, glancing over at her. "This is the last stop."

"What? The car?"

"Think about it. We've probably spent more time together here than anywhere else in the world. How many nights have we just driven around for hours 'cause there's nothing else to do?"

She knows it's true. For all the memories of these past two years, this is how she'll probably think of him most often: his hand slung loosely over the wheel, a lazy smile on his face, the music filling the air around them.

"You're right," she says, letting her eyes flutter shut for a moment.

He reaches out and pokes her. "Don't fall asleep on me now. We've made it this far."

Her eyes flash open again. "But no farther," she says, the words slipping out before she has a chance to think better of them.

Aidan looks at her sideways, a question behind his eyes.

"It's just...I heard what you said to your dad."

"About what?"

"About us. He asked if we were staying together, and you said no. Remember?"

Aidan frowns. "Is this a trick question?"

"No."

"Well...I thought we decided that hours ago. *You* decided it."

"I know," she says, shifting to face him. "We did. But it

222

was the way you said it. Like it was nothing. Like *we* were nothing."

He readjusts his grip on the wheel. "Look, I'm sorry if I did something wrong, but I thought we were both on the same page here. I thought we'd decided—"

"But that was before," she says in a small voice.

"Before what?"

"Before I said it."

"Said—" he begins, then stops short. "Oh."

Clare stares at her knees. There's a patch over one of them, and she almost laughs, because Aidan is the only person she knows who would mend a pair of sweatpants. He hates to give up on anything.

"I'm sorry," she says, when she can't stand the silence any longer. "I guess I shouldn't have expected that it would change anything. I'm not even sure I want it to, but hearing you say it to your dad like that...I don't know. Something about it seemed so simple. You made it sound almost easy."

"Clare," he says, easing the car onto the side of the road in front of a house that looks like all the others, with flowerpots and a basketball hoop and a wooden mailbox. "There's nothing easy about this. This is the hardest thing I've ever done. And the worst part is...it's just the beginning. This is going to be hard every single minute of every single day for a really long time."

This time, she doesn't stop herself. She reaches over and lays a hand on top of his. His face is clouded over, but his eyes, when he looks up at her, are very clear. She wants to say: *It doesn't have to be this hard.* She wants to say: *It's not too late to change our minds.* But instead, she just says: "I know."

"We decided this for a reason. All that stuff you were saying before. About how we should be jumping into our new lives with both feet..."

"That makes it sound like hopscotch," she says, pulling her hand back.

"Okay, well, maybe it was something about diving in. Or was that my thing? I don't remember exactly. The point is that you had a whole list of reasons. Remember?"

Clare nods miserably.

"And you know this obviously wasn't what I wanted—or at least it isn't what I *thought* I wanted. But now? I don't know. I actually think you might be right."

As she listens to him, it starts to feel like there's something heavy on her chest. She takes a few shallow breaths. "I'm not always right, you know."

He laughs. "Yes, you are."

"But what if I'm wrong about *this*? What if the hardest thing isn't breaking up? What if it's staying together—making this work in spite of the distance, in spite of everything—and that's what we're supposed to be doing?"

"Clare—"

"No, seriously. What if I'm being a complete idiot and just playing it safe like I always do?" She's aware of the slightly hysterical tinge to her voice, but she's powerless to stop it. "What if I'm really just ruining everything?"

He gives her a steady look, his eyes full of a warmth that makes this all so much worse. "But what if you're not?" he asks quietly. "I think maybe it's true, what you said before—that we can either end things on our own terms now or let it fizzle out. And I sort of feel like I have this responsibility to—I don't know—not let you get caught up in the moment and decide the wrong thing."

She feels suddenly weary. Out the window, the sun is tinting the street a shade of orange so bright it doesn't seem real, a wash of color so brilliant it almost hurts.

"Look," he says, ducking his head and rubbing at the back of his neck. "You're my best friend. And my family. You're my whole life, really."

"Aidan—"

"So this thing between us? It's way too important to let it just fall apart. I don't want to break up in a few days or weeks or months for some really dumb reason. We're not that couple. If we're gonna break up, it can't be because of the guy always hanging around your dorm room or because I'm sitting by my phone and you're never calling, or because I'm too busy with lacrosse to text you back, and it starts driving you nuts. If we're gonna break up, it has to be for a good reason."

She shakes her head. "I can't think of a single good reason to break up with you right now."

"That's because you're not thinking big enough," he says. "It's gotta be something huge, something grand."

"Like world peace?"

"If world peace were a possible side effect of you breaking up with me, then yes, sure, that would definitely count as a noble reason."

"Maybe," she says after a moment, "it's just that we love each other too much."

He looks at her thoughtfully. "I like that."

"But it's still a bullshit reason."

"It's actually the opposite of bullshit. We love each other too much to get dragged down by any bullshit. We're *above* bullshit. What's the scientific term for that? Not *sub*, but..."

"*Super*," she says. "It's super bullshit."

"Super Bullshit: worst superhero ever," he says with a laugh, but Clare only stares at the patch on her knee with a sinking heart.

"So that's it, then?" she asks, and he nods.

"That's our reason: We dove each other way too much."

She rolls her eyes. "That was only cute once."

He grins. "So was the whole *I dove you* thing in the first place."

"Fair enough," she says. "But I do."

"Dove me?"

"Love you," she says, waiting for him to smile again. But he doesn't. Instead, he looks at her for a long time, his eyes taking her in as if trying to memorize her. Then, finally, he nods.

"Seems like a worthy reason to me."

STOP #16

The End

6:24 AM

Aidan is still sitting exactly where Clare left him: in one of the huge wooden rocking chairs on the front porch. When she steps outside, Bingo shoves past her through the open door, charging over to greet him with a dramatic display of wiggling and whining before launching himself up into his lap.

Aidan wrestles the dog into a hug, then glances up at Clare.

"Were they mad?" he asks, looking a little worried. He's grown accustomed to disappointing his own father, but Clare's parents hold him in such high esteem that he's made it his mission to prove that they're right about him.

"About what?" she asks, sitting down in the other chair. From inside the house, she can still hear the muffled voices of her parents calling back and forth to each other as they make last-minute preparations for the drive, gathering snacks and road maps and water bottles. The trip will take four days: two heading east with all three of them, and then another two returning west after having dropped her off in New Hampshire.

"Well," Aidan says, scratching Bingo behind the ears, "the black eye, for one."

Clare shrugs. "I told them I joined a fight club."

"Seriously."

"Seriously? I just told them the truth."

He shakes his head. "I always forget that's an option."

"They weren't thrilled, obviously, but there's not much to do about it now. My mom's running around trying to find some makeup to pack, so I don't look quite so intimidating when I show up to meet Beatrice St. James."

"And they didn't care that you were out all night?"

"Nah," she says, pushing back so that her chair beats a low, thumping rhythm on the hollow slats of the porch. It's fully light now, but the sun is hidden behind the clouds, which are low and heavy, a scrim of gray across the horizon. "They told me that, starting tomorrow, I'll be free to stay out all night every night without them knowing, so it's just as well I got a head start."

Aidan laughs. "I had that exact same argument all ready for my parents. I guess yours are a step ahead of even me."

Above them, a bird lands on the roof, making little scratching noises as it hops across the shingles, and Bingo goes stiff at the sound, letting out a single warning bark before burying himself in the crook of Aidan's elbow again. The rain has returned, or is about to; the air is heavy with the scent of it, and in the distance, there's a long rumble of thunder. It almost feels to Clare like the world is holding its breath.

"Remember that time we watched the storm out here?" she asks, and Aidan's hand goes still over the dog's soft coat, his eyes creasing at the corners as he calls up the memory.

"That lightning was crazy," he says. "It lit up the entire block."

"And the whole house was shaking from the thunder."

"And you wanted to go inside. . . ."

"No, I didn't," she says, but when he arches an eyebrow, she gives in. "Okay, maybe. But only because we were getting soaked." She leans her head back against the wooden chair and stares up at the eaves of the porch. "I'm really gonna miss this."

"The rain?" Aidan says. "I'm pretty sure they'll have some at Dartmouth."

"Not the rain," she says, sitting up again. "All the rest of it. Of this."

"I know," he says. "Me too."

"I've been thinking..." she says, curling her fingers around the arms of the chair, trying to work up the resolve to say what needs to be said. "I wonder if this would all be easier if we didn't talk for a little while."

She braves a glance in Aidan's direction in time to see his eyes flash with surprise. "Really? That's what you want?"

"I wouldn't say I *want* it," Clare says. "But this is gonna be hard enough as it is. And if we're really trying to move on, which we probably should, then maybe there's something to be said for all or nothing."

She glances down to where she's been chipping at a cracked piece of paint on the chair without even realizing it, picking it clean off like a scab. When she looks up again, Aidan is watching her, and she has to steel herself before continuing, her voice cracking a little on the words. "I mean...how am I ever supposed to stop missing you if you're only a phone call away?"

He nods, absently patting the dog, who is nearly asleep on his lap now. "I guess that makes sense," he says with a frown. "But it just seems so...final."

"Well, it wouldn't be forever—"

"I hope not," he interrupts her, looking stricken.

"—but maybe just for a little while. Until we get used to this."

He lets out a humorless laugh. "I feel like you just took away my security blanket or something. This whole thing was a lot easier to get my head around when I thought I could still call you tonight."

"Yeah, but see? That's the problem. We'll never move on if we're still talking all the time."

He rubs at his forehead. "I know. You're right. But still."

"It won't be so bad," she says, though she feels nervous even at the thought of it. "We'll just have to quit each other cold turkey."

"Is that code for 'until Thanksgiving'?" he asks with a weak smile.

"I don't know," she says. "Maybe. It actually kind of makes sense, since it'll be the next time we see each other in person. And it'll give us enough time to really try at school, you know? To make a real effort to live our own lives without depending on each other all the time."

"Yeah," Aidan says, "but it's about a million years away."

Clare smiles. "It's three months."

"That's a long time."

"It'll go fast," she promises, but he only shakes his head.

"Not fast enough."

Beyond the edges of the porch, the rain arrives all at once, sweeping over the house in a fine mist that sends Bingo scrambling off Aidan's lap and over to the door, where he scratches insistently. Clare is about to get up and let him in when her mother appears, and the dog goes flying inside without a backward glance.

"Ten-minute warning, you two," she says, poking her head out and giving Aidan a little wave. She glances over at Clare, who is still wearing his oversize sweats. "Uh, were you gonna change...?"

"I'm okay," she says. "We'll be in soon."

Once they're alone again, Clare can still feel Aidan watching her, but now his mouth is twisted up in an effort not to laugh.

"What?" she asks, tucking her feet up beneath her.

"Nothing. It's just a good look for you. And the perfume is nice, too."

"Perfume?"

"We stink," he says with a grin. "Like fish."

Clare rolls her eyes. "My parents won't care. And we're staying in a hotel tonight, so it's just for the car ride." She tugs on the drawstrings of the hoodie. "But just for that, you're not getting this back."

What she can't bear to say is that, really, she just wants an excuse to keep him close.

"Shouldn't be too hard to find another UCLA sweatshirt at UCLA," he says, and then he shakes his head in wonder. "I can't believe I'll be there later today."

"I know," Clare says. "It's so weird. I've looked at a million pictures of Dartmouth, but it's still hard to imagine actually being there."

"I can picture it," Aidan says, squeezing his eyes shut. "I'm seeing leaves. Lots and lots of leaves." He opens one eye to look at her. "Is it always fall at Dartmouth? I think every picture I've ever seen has some sort of foliage."

"Yes, it's always fall at Dartmouth."

He closes his eyes again. "Just what I thought. And I always imagine you sitting on a bench, for some reason, under a tree with a million different-colored leaves—"

"Even purple?"

"Sure, why not?" he says. "And you'll just be sitting there with your bag of books and your cup of coffee and your fall coat, thinking important, college-y thoughts."

"I have a feeling," Clare says with a little smile, "that what I'll actually be thinking about is you."

"At first, yeah," Aidan says, looking over at her with a

more somber expression. "But not later. Trust me on this. The day will come when you'll be sitting there looking up at the sky, and you won't be thinking of me at all. You won't need to anymore. And it'll be a good thing, because it means you'll be happy."

"I don't know," she says quietly. "That's pretty hard to imagine."

Aidan only smiles. "You'll see," he says, closing his eyes again as he listens to the rain. Clare watches him for a moment, desperately trying to collect all the little pieces of him that she hopes to take with her: the freckles on the tips of his ears, his pale eyelashes, the curve of his hairline, even the half-moon bruises beneath each eye.

"There's a third option, you know," she says, and when he moves his head to the side, his eyes take a second to focus.

"To what?"

"To us," she says, her heart straining hard against her rib cage. "We keep tossing around these two possibilities: End things now or let it fizzle out. But there's a third option."

"What," he asks with a wry smile, "happily ever after?"

"No," she says quickly. "Come on. I'm serious."

He raises his arms in a stretch. "Okay, then what?"

"Later."

"There is no later," he says, holding out his wrist. He taps twice on the glass face of his watch. "Time's a-ticking."

"No, that's the third possibility," she says, her words nearly lost to the hum of the rain, which has wrapped the porch in a glossy curtain. "That we'll come back to each other later."

Aidan's eyes are fixed on her, and there's something hopeful in his gaze, something expectant. "Yeah?"

"Yeah," she says. "After we've learned some stuff and done some things. We keep thinking there are only these two choices: We either grow apart or grow together. But maybe we can just kind of each grow on our own, and see how it goes. And then later, if it's right, we'll come back to each other and start again."

"Later," he says, as if testing the word.

She nods. "Later."

"Like a second prologue."

"There's no such thing," she says, shaking her head, but this doesn't seem to bother him. He only smiles.

"Who says?"

This time, when the door swings open behind them, they both know what it means. Clare's stomach drops, and she can see a flicker of alarm in Aidan's eyes.

"Sorry to interrupt," her mom says from the doorway, her voice full of apology. "But it's time to load the car."

Even after they've stood up, the chairs continue to rock back and forth, and the rain continues to fall all around the porch, shimmering and insistent. Aidan manages a small smile just before they walk inside, but when Clare tries to match it, she can't.

The time has come, and there's no more outrunning it.

Inside, her dad is walking down the stairs with a cardboard box. But when he notices them, he sets it down, his eyes widening as he catches sight of Aidan's face.

"You look worse than Clare," he says, reaching out to shake his hand.

"I know," her mom says, glancing worriedly at Aidan. "We have some frozen corn, if you want to grab a bag."

"Corn?" her dad scoffs. "Come on. At least give the boy a steak or something. It's clearly been a rough night."

Clare's mom rolls her eyes. "You're welcome to whatever you'd like," she says, patting Aidan on the shoulder as she moves around him to the stairs. "You know that." Just before walking up, she turns around once more, and this time, her voice quivers a little bit. "You're *always* welcome here."

Right then, the thing that kills Clare the most is that her mom doesn't even know yet. When she'd dashed inside before to tell them she was home, she couldn't bear to let them know it was over. It would only make it more real.

Besides, she figures they have hours ahead of them for all that, hours when she'll stare out the car window and tell them all the reasons why this makes sense, why it was the logical thing to do—ending things with Aidan—in the hope that if she just keeps explaining, it might keep her from crying.

Though, of course, it won't.

But now she realizes that her mom doesn't need to be

told after all; she already seems to know. And Clare is grateful for that, because it means she won't actually have to say the words later. Instead, she can curl up in the backseat and let her mom pass her juice boxes and let her dad find something upbeat on the radio as they drive through Illinois and then Indiana and then Ohio, and on and on to New Hampshire, putting the miles between her and Aidan one at a time, until the moment when his flight takes off, and the distance between them will all at once be too great to count.

For the next ten minutes, the four of them troop in and out of the house, Bingo at their heels, as they carry suitcases and shopping bags, cardboard boxes of various sizes, pillows and lamps and even a football.

"Since when do you play football?" Aidan asks when he sees Clare walking through the kitchen with it tucked under her arm. He whisks it away from her, then stands near the sink, flipping it over and over in his hands.

"I don't know," she says with a shrug. "I feel like it's the kind of thing you do in college. You know, toss a football around on the quad. Or is that Hacky Sack?"

He throws the ball to her, a gentle toss that spirals over the kitchen table, but somehow she still manages to fumble it.

"There goes my college athletic career," she says, bending to grab the ball. "But I'm still bringing it."

"When I said you should try some new things," Aidan says, "I wasn't really talking about contact sports."

"Yeah, well, you won't be laughing when I come back a seasoned quarterback."

"Now *that* I'd like to see," he says as they walk outside together.

In the driveway, her dad is shutting the trunk of the car. He's wearing a bright yellow slicker with the hood pulled up, and his glasses are speckled with rain.

"I think that's pretty much everything," he says. "Unless you want to take the kitchen sink, too."

"Very funny," Clare says, but already there's a lump in her throat, because she would, if she could: She'd rip that stupid, leaky sink right out of the wall and take it with her. For a brief, surging, impossible moment, she wants it all: her dog and her bed and her parents and her boyfriend. Even now, with just minutes to go, she has no idea how she's going to leave any of it behind.

Her mom steps outside with the end of Bingo's leash in one hand and a plastic bag full of sandwiches in the other. She locks the door and then turns around, staring at the odd rain-soaked trio assembled in the driveway, all of them looking back at her with obvious reluctance.

"I guess we're all set," she says, glancing down at the dog. Bingo is holding his leash in his mouth and wagging his tail, completely oblivious to the fact that they'll be dropping him off at the kennel on their way out of town. "This is it, huh?

Her dad nods a bit too enthusiastically. "The start of a big adventure."

"We'll just give you two a minute," her mom says, then walks over to Aidan, standing on her tiptoes to give him a quick hug.

"We'll miss you," she says. "Good luck out there, okay?"

"Okay," Aidan manages. "And thanks for everything."

Her dad claps him on the shoulder, which turns into a hug. "Take care of yourself."

Aidan nods. "Drive safe."

And then they're getting into the car, the engine rumbling to life and the windshield wipers squealing, and Clare is struck by a panic so strong that she feels her heart might gallop straight out of her chest.

This is it, she thinks, frozen in place. Even after all these hours—all these months, really—she's still oddly stunned to have arrived here in this moment, which feels like it's happening both much too fast and far too slowly.

She wipes some rain out of her eyes and forces herself to look up at Aidan, who is standing a few feet away from her, his face pale and his eyes filled with dread.

"Last chance to run away together," he says, attempting a smile, though there's something wobbly about it. "I hear Canada is nice this time of year."

"I think I'd prefer the desert island."

"Even if I refuse to wear a hula skirt?"

"Even then," she says, reaching out to take his hand, terrified about what happens next. Because how do you say goodbye to a piece of yourself? She examines his hand, tracing a finger over his palm, playing connect-the-dots with the constellation of freckles on his wrist. "This is the worst, huh?"

"It's definitely not the best."

"Do you think we'll be miserable?"

"Yes," he says simply. "For a while, anyway."

"And then?"

"And then it'll get easier."

"Promise?"

"No," he says with a feeble smile. "So...really no contact at all?"

For a moment, she wants desperately to take it back. Because it's hard to imagine not being able to text him on the drive out there, not being able to call after she meets Beatrice, not getting messages from him between classes. But she knows this is the way it has to be, and so, with great effort, she shakes her head.

Aidan nods. "No phone calls?"

"Nope."

"Texts?"

"Nope."

"E-mails? Letters? Postcards?"

"Sorry."

"Carrier pigeons?"

"Oh, sure," she says. "Pigeons are totally fine."

"Well, at least there's something," he says with a grin.

"Aidan," she says, grabbing the front of his shirt and giving it a little tug. Somewhere inside her, an army of tears is on the move, the pressure building behind her eyes and in her throat. Soon, it will be too much. Whatever dams might exist—whatever walls she's managed to throw up—will surely break, and all the many hollows of her heart will be flooded. It takes all her strength to fight against it, because there are still things to be said, and she can't bear for them to be muddled.

But even this seems beyond her at the moment.

"I don't..." she begins, but quickly falters.

Aidan only nods. "Me neither."

"I wish..."

"I know," he says. "Me too."

She gives up then, stepping into his arms and resting her head against his chest, but then she hears the soft thud of his heart, and she knows there's only one thing left that matters. "I love you," she says, the words clear and steady and true, and she can hear the smile in his voice as he says it back: "And I dove you."

"Shut up," she says, but they're both laughing a little bit now. When she tilts her head back, he kisses her for the last time, and all she can think is that this is another kind of first, something she hadn't counted when she made her list: their first goodbye.

"Have a good trip," he says as they pull apart again, and this—finally—is what tips her over the edge. She can't help it: She begins to cry, swiping uselessly at the tears, but unable to stop, because it's such an ordinary thing to say in a moment that feels so fantastically unreal.

But when it's her turn, she can do no better. "I'll miss

you," she tells him, holding on for a second more, though the car is puffing out clouds of exhaust, and the rain is coming down harder all around them, and the end of all this—the end of them—is finally here after all this time, rushing up to meet them like a freight train, noisy and unstoppable, the sound of it loud in her ears.

Aidan kisses her once more on the top of her head, and she clings to his hand for another few seconds before letting go. When she finally does, she can't bear to look, or she's certain she might never actually leave, and so instead, she squares her shoulders and breathes in and out, walking straight over to the car and climbing inside with her heart skidding around in her chest and the tears all mixed up with the rain on her face.

"You okay?" her mom asks, once she's shut the door, but Clare has no idea how to answer that, because she is and she isn't, because she's stuck somewhere between the end and the beginning, and the only way to get unstuck, it seems, is to keep moving.

So she nods. "Let's go," she says as Bingo clambers onto her lap, his tail fanning the air. Her dad throws the car into gear, and they back out of the driveway with the dog looking out the rain-streaked window as they pass Aidan, because Clare can't seem to bring herself to do it. But once they're on the street, she changes her mind, struck by an urgent need to see him one more time, so she twists around in her seat, peering between the boxes piled in back.

He's still there, of course, standing in the rain as he

watches them go. It almost feels to Clare like she left a piece of her heart back there with him, the two halves being stretched between them like taffy. She lifts a hand, and he does the same, and they remain like that for what feels like a very long time, fixed in a slow-motion version of goodbye.

In another kind of story, Clare knows, this would be different. If this were a movie, she'd yell for her dad to stop the car, and then, amid the screech of the brakes and the squeal of the tires, she'd go hurtling out the door, running down the rain-soaked street, desperate to tell Aidan one last thing before she goes.

But the truth is there's nothing more to say. Over the past twelve hours, they've spent all their words—generously, riotously, fully—like a couple of gamblers throwing down every last chip without a single thought for tomorrow.

And now, she knows, the only thing left for them to do is to go out and find some more stories to tell, to start a brand-new collection of adventures and memories, to keep them close like the best of all souvenirs, and then one day, if they're really lucky, to find a way to bring them home again.

PROLOGUE

At the mail center, the man behind the counter scans Clare's receipt before disappearing into the back room to retrieve the box. Behind her, the line is long, and everyone seems restless, but nobody more than Clare, who stands on her tiptoes, craning to see what it is that someone sent her.

It's not that she never gets mail; when you go to school a couple of hours from the nearest major city, you end up doing most of your shopping online. But since starting here last fall, she can count on one hand the number of unexpected packages she's received.

There were two from her mother back in September, not long after she first arrived: one filled with candy and photos, the other with a few things she'd accidentally left behind. And then a couple for her birthday in October, including one from Stella that contained an old dictionary with words like *confidant* and *rapport* and *camaraderie* carefully circled throughout. (Clare suspected they were more than just suggestions for enhancing her vocabulary.)

But that's pretty much it.

So when the man finally returns with a square box, heaving it onto the counter, Clare has to keep herself from reaching for it while he checks her name off a form.

"Rocks?" he asks, raising his eyebrows as he scribbles something.

"Huh?"

"Someone sending you rocks?"

Clare shakes her head. "I don't think so."

"Sure feels like it," he says, pushing it over to her, and when she picks it up, she realizes that he's right. It's heavier than it looks, and she readjusts her grip, her fingers slipping beneath the weight of it.

She makes it all the way to the end of the crowded hallway before she allows herself to look at the return label, though by that point, she doesn't need to. The moment she picked up the box, she knew exactly who it was from and what was inside.

Even so, it nearly takes her breath away when she sees Aidan's familiar handwriting in the upper-left-hand corner of the box. Beside the return address, he's crossed out the word *FedEx* with a thick black marker and written *carrier pigeon* instead.

She hasn't heard a word from him in five months. Not since that first night back home over Thanksgiving.

And now, there's this: a box appearing as if from nowhere, as if by magic.

Someone bumps her elbow, and she fumbles it a little, catching it with her knee. She realizes she's still standing in the middle of the hallway, so she forces herself to walk up the stairs, weaving through dozens of students on the way to class—nodding here and there at the ones she knows—and cradling the box as if it were something fragile, though she's already sure it's not.

Outside the building, she hurries over to a bench, then sits with the package balanced on her lap, staring at the address. It takes a long time for her heart to slow down. Just the sight of Aidan's name has sent her spinning, and she tips her head back to look up at the sky, trying to collect herself again.

It had been like this over Thanksgiving, too: Seeing him there in her driveway after three whole months apart, three whole months of silence, was enough to make her dizzy. With his clear blue eyes and the reddish stubble along his jaw, he looked completely different and yet also staggeringly, heartbreakingly familiar.

It only took a moment for everything else to fall away: all the words she'd planned to say to him, all the things she'd been waiting to tell him.

One of them, most of all: that she was seeing someone new.

But before they even had a chance to say hello, before they'd even exchanged a word, Aidan was kissing her, right there in the driveway, and suddenly that didn't seem so important anymore. In fact, it seemed like the least important thing in the world.

It wasn't until after they broke apart and she saw the look in his eyes—a look that matched her own, stuck somewhere between longing and regret—that she realized he was seeing someone, too.

They hadn't talked after that. She avoided him for the rest of the break, started a thousand e-mails to him once she returned to school, let her thumb hover over his name on her phone too many times to count. But it seemed better to leave it alone. They'd both moved on. They'd known it might happen. It was the way things were supposed to go.

Over Christmas, he stayed in California, which she only knew because Riley had mentioned it in an e-mail, how she and her parents were going out there to visit him. Clare couldn't help wondering if he was trying to steer clear of her, though she knew it was much more likely he was staying out there to be with his new girlfriend. It would be weeks yet before she'd break up with her own boyfriend, but still, something about the thought of Aidan's sunshine-filled holiday made her feel horribly lonely.

When she returned home over break, she let herself walk past his darkened house only once. She stood there for a long time, the snow falling all around her, remembering that night in the driveway, their last one together, and then she turned around and left.

Now she blinks up at the branches of a towering elm

tree. The leaves no longer look like they did when she first arrived here, like they do in all the brochures: wild with color, an electric palette of reds and yellows and oranges. Instead, they're green and new, and they smell like spring. Above them, the sun is a white dot in the cloudless sky, and the air is cool and brisk. Everything is so bright and dazzling it hardly seems real.

Clare looks down at the box again, then slides a fingernail under the tape at the corner. When she rips it off, it makes a sawing noise, and she pulls back the flaps to see what's inside, what she'd known from the minute she'd picked it up would be inside: tucked in a nest of newspaper like an oversize egg, there's a bright green bowling ball.

She laughs as she runs a hand over the smooth, marbled surface. In the sunlight, the color is brilliant, emerald green and as shiny as a precious gem. She can't help wondering if he bought it or stole it, thinking back to their conversation all those months ago, when he reminded her that the hardest things are the ones most worth doing.

She has a feeling that it's stolen, and she loves it all the more for that.

Just as she's about to fold up the box again, she notices something else: a flash of white in the midst of all that green. In one of the three circular holes, there's a rolled-up piece of paper, and she hesitates for a moment, marveling at the possibilities. Just seeing it there is enough to rattle her, to make her rubber-band heart snap back into place again, the twang of it jangling straight down through her toes.

She sits there for a long time, for what feels like forever, and then, when she's finally ready, she removes the note gingerly, using both hands to flatten the page.

All it says is this: *Is it later yet?*

And here's the amazing thing: Now it was.

ACKNOWLEDGMENTS

A great big thank-you to Jennifer Joel, Farrin Jacobs, Elizabeth Bewley, Megan Tingley, Andrew Smith, Hallie Patterson, Josie Freedman, Sophie Harris, Imogen Taylor, Binky Urban, Kelly Mitchell, Sarah Mlynowski, Ryan Doherty, Liz Casal, Maggie Edkins, Leslie Shumate, Madeleine Osborn, Emilie Polster, Barbara Bakowski, JoAnna Kremer, Libby McGuire, Jennifer Hershey, Mark Tavani, and Jenni Hamill. I'd also like to thank everyone at LBYR, Curtis Brown, Headline, and Random House for their support. And, of course, my family: Dad, Mom, Kelly, and Errol.